SAVERIO

A TALE OF THE VAMPIRE

M. KATHLEEN ROBBINS

Library of Congress Registration Number:
Txu 2-127-293

eBook Version: **ISBN-13: 978-1-7340905-1-2**
Print Version: **ISBN-13: 978-1-7340905-0-5**

This story is entirely a work of fiction and all characters, except historical
figures are purely a product of the author's imagination. The resemblance of
any character in this work to persons living or dead is purely coincidental.

Nothing in the story as relates to historical figures is taken from life except in
the broadest sense.

It's all made up.

But, I am told it is a pretty good story and I hope you enjoy it.

~

With love and many thanks to my supporters, Andy, Sarah and Calvin, my helper, Bella, my willing reader, Tristen, my first fan, Trent, and my biggest cheerleader, Russ.

For my champion, Gary

*And in loving memory of **Jess**, the bravest of all the demon fighters*

~

CONTENTS

CHAPTER 1
THE INTERLOPER

A damp touch from an ebony crypt,
The kiss, Nosferatu's grim troth of terror
Conjures an abandonment of innocence
And, by and by, creeps back below the sunken earth.

E velina held her breath. The intruder, that she had prayed would not show his face at her nuptial feast, was now crossing the makeshift dance floor of the social hall. His eyes were ablaze with green fire and his mocking smile showed perfectly even, sharp, white teeth. Panic rose under the satin bodice of Evelina's unadorned but elegant gown, cutting off her breath. Her heart beat wildly. The room swayed around her.

Waiting for this day, she had hoped against hope there would be no interference from this man who was no longer a man at all. He had once, some years ago, held her life in his hands and preserved it. In that way, he had made this dreamed-of day possible. She could not quite believe that he would use her for ill now. Another side of her feared that this was the exact day for which he had been waiting. She also felt uneasy about the safety of those who were laughing, drinking, and celebrating around her. Her precious husband of two hours knew nothing of the existence of the invading wretch. Evelina was aware that her groom's ignorance made him every bit as vulnerable as their guests. She had wanted to believe that her family and the other invitees would be safe at a celebration held this close to a holy sanctuary. Yet, here was the brute in the cold flesh.

The guests parted, making way for the uninvited caller as he strode through the crowd. Not one of them turned to look at the thin, pale man. His open black coat swayed around him as he marched a straight path toward Evelina. He did not pause until he was within inches of her, looming over her so closely that she could see the stitches of his silky, white shirt. The modest train of her dress prevented her from stepping too hastily backward. As she twisted her torso and attempted to gather up the folds of satin, the creature spun around to stand beside her, his back to the decorated table covered with its sumptuous banquet. As the two of them faced the roomful of boisterous celebrants, the invader grabbed Evelina's right arm, hard, just above the elbow. The man was discreet in his threatening machinations. He held his frame in such a way as to disguise the fact that he had tight hold of the bride. Evelina, doing her best not to cause a scene in this place, on this important day, willed herself not to cry out from the pressure of the animal's grip. With considerable effort, she maintained her smile as her wide, brown eyes searched the room for the ally who would understand this situation and come to her aid.

When she spotted him in the crowd, Father Ennio appeared to be doing his best to make his way to her and her frosty companion without drawing undue attention. Evelina saw her friend artfully step in front of the young man who had been engaged to follow the bride and her guests with his camera. The unwanted, if not altogether unexpected, trespasser would not be visible in a photograph or even be seen through a lens. Evelina hoped her other guests were too busy enjoying themselves to be watching her as she pulled against the unnatural strength of the demon's grip. It was like trying to pull away a limb encased in concrete.

The aggressor's heart did not beat, yet the nearness of him made Evelina's race with fear and, as much as she hated to acknowledge it, desire. She believed Ennio when he said these feelings were due to a fascination created by the ogre's hypnotic power. It was comforting knowledge, but the idea of being under the spell of the Nosferatu was nonetheless alarming.

"You haven't been invited here, Saverio," admonished the good Father as he reached the scene of the drama. "How typical of you to materialize where you are least wanted."

"Ah, but this beautiful bride is not at all typical. She is the reason I have come," sneered Saverio.

Ennio was ready with his answer and began speaking over the top of Saverio's final words. "Oh, I am well aware of your obsession with Evelina," he scoffed. "I am sure you would not lie to me old friend." The sarcasm of his tone was barely distinguishable beneath the calm, quiet way he spoke. Nothing but his emphasis on the word, "friend," gave away his insincerity. "But know that she has given each bridesmaid a silver crucifix to wear today," he warned, "just in case you are trying to divert our attention."

"Are the groomsmen protected as well?" taunted Saverio. "A woman's blood is a tantalizing mix of sweet and tart. It is full of the potency of her creative force, her femininity, and her awesome strength. A man's blood, by contrast, is laced with testosterone. It provides another type of fire, uncontrolled and reckless! If I were here to feast, like the lot of you," the monster waved his free arm to indicate the room full of revelers, "it would not matter to me if my quarry were women or men." He paused, then added with a smirk as his emerald eyes swept the joyful crowd, "or children; you know that, priest."

Evelina stood motionless throughout this exchange. She said nothing, trusting Ennio to make a move that might afford her escape. At the mention of feasting on children, the cleric immediately pressed his hand into Saverio's arm. It was a gesture that would likely be seen by an onlooker as a warm greeting. Saverio made a sound like a snake about to strike and loosened his iron grip. Evelina spun away from him to stand behind Ennio and saw the wooden crucifix in the priest's hand.

"Leave this place, Saverio," commanded Ennio. "I too can hunt, you know."

"I came to wish the glorious bride a long and blissful married life," replied Saverio. His glowing, viridian eyes were fixed steadily on Evelina's face. "I will go when I have kissed her goodbye." Evelina tried to look over Saverio's shoulder and focus on a portrait of the newly installed Pope John

XXIII on the far wall, but the fiend's electric green orbs pulled her velvety, fawn eyes to him.

Ennio reached for Evelina's arm as she, transfixed, moved around him and slid into Saverio's embrace.

The venomous dark angel leaned his head to the bride's mouth. She felt the sting of his razor-edged teeth as he stroked her lips with his. She tasted blood and waves of passion engulfed her. Father Ennio, maintaining his composure for one more moment, pulled her back to him with a deft motion.

Evelina turned to see her benefactor's eyes narrow with vexation he could no longer repress. He spat, "Get out now Saverio or the end of this cross is going through your heart."

Saverio chuckled contemptuously. "You wouldn't, not here. But I will go, little man, just as I said I would. Save your cross for your prayers. You will need it." The wild, green eyes narrowed as he leaned in toward Ennio. "You will need those prayers much more than even *you* know, priest." The interloper stood taller, turned his head, lifted his chin and sniffed the air.

Evelina watched, eyes wide as Saverio slowly turned. When her eyes began to burn and water, she blinked twice and he was gone. It was as if he had never been there. Evelina surveyed the room but caught only the hint of a shadow as it passed by the stained-glass church window. She had learned from ancient tomes Ennio had given her to read that vampires eschewed even pale sunlight, unless they were particularly well-fed. With the late day sun lingering low in the western sky, she prayed that none of the guests who had attended her afternoon wedding were missing.

CHAPTER 2
THE HARBINGER

Beelzebub's macabre creation
Arises from diabolical, cringing madness
To consign terror
And obliterate all hope.

Father Ennio was indeed, a person of small stature. Nevertheless, he was a man of great inner fortitude. He recaptured his calm with a single deep breath and commenced running interference for Evelina. He intercepted guests making their way toward the bride, allowing her to escape to the water closet in the sacristy of the aged Roman chapel. The dignified and appealing church, one of the nine hundred or so in the city, was connected to its social hall, full of merrymakers, by a short breezeway. The sacristy, a private, hidden room behind the altar, was a secluded area where Ennio and his curate prepared for Mass, just as hundreds had before them. The simple rectangular space was cool and peaceful. Along one wall ecclesiastical robes hung in careful order. Tall racks of wine-filled bottles stood in an arched niche. A wide variety of candelabra were lined up in a neat row on an eye-level shelf. Attached to the bottom of the shelf were hooks for holding the patens used by altar boys during Holy Communion. In a back corner, a tall, white door opened into the compact bathroom. Here, Evelina could rinse her mouth and calm her breathing, secure in the knowledge that no evil thing could get past the alcove that held the body of Christ. The texts were ambiguous about some vampiric characteristics but they were clear about the danger even a single sanctified wafer posed to Saverio's kind. A vampire could burst into flames trying to get to Evelina in her sanctuary, behind the chalice of hosts in the tabernacle. *That is something I would pay to see right this minute*, she mused.

As she ran water into the sink and dabbed at her bottom lip with a white hand towel, Evelina considered her decision to be married in a public ceremony. She reminded herself that Saverio could come and go almost imperceptibly when he chose to – no matter the venue. But, for reasons known only to the monster himself, he had made himself known to Evelina again and again. She and Ennio were positive that the ghoul kept track of her movements and would surely know if Evelina and her fiancé tried to elope. Ennio had suggested that the couple be married in a place where he, the body of Christ, and the Holy Spirit could offer some protection. Gaetano happily agreed to the big church wedding and full Mass that Evelina's mother would have wanted for her.

The church was a holy place. The social hall, on the other hand, was a public area like any other. Evelina had learned today that it did not provide enough protection via routine blessings to keep Saverio at bay. Her one, pitiful consolation was that after he had created his opportunity to upset and frighten her, Saverio had said he was going. Evelina hoped with all of her heart that he meant it.

Feeling ashamed of her inward reaction to the vampire's kiss, and unnerved by his presence among those she loved, Evelina prayed. She said an act of contrition, then repeated the petitions she had been reciting for weeks. She begged God, the Holy Mother, St. Michael and anyone who might be listening for the safety of all present at her reception and all who could become victims of Saverio, or any vampire, in Rome and around the world.

By the time she had finished her appeal, the bleeding of her bottom lip had stopped. Evelina patted her face and around her eyes with the damp cloth and made herself take several slow, deep breaths. Still feeling a little bit shaky but knowing Ennio would start to worry soon, she practiced her smile in the mirror once and then emerged from her safe cocoon. It was her wedding day, she reasoned. No one would find it suspicious if her face were a bit red, her manner excited, or even if she were trembling a wee bit.

When she arrived back in the hall, she observed Ennio, as nonplussed as ever after a brush with pure depravity, at the long table of food and refreshment. He was filling another plate with all manner of delectable, wedding-day treats. *How does he face the devil with such calm?* Evelina wondered for the dozenth time as he tossed her a little wave with the pastry he held in his hand.

A moment later, the authentically blushing bride spied her new husband on the dance floor. She recognized the woman with whom he was dancing as a cousin of his. Evelina had met the pretty young woman at one or two family gatherings, but could not quite recall her name. Gaetano was nodding in agreement with whatever the woman was saying as his flashing blue eyes scanned the room.

When he caught sight of Evelina, he cocked his head in a gesture that she knew meant, "Are you alright?" Evelina smiled what she hoped was an appropriately festive smile and nodded.

One of the tall and attractive groomsmen who worked alongside Gaetano at a large bank near Vatican City stopped Evelina and politely requested a dance. She was somewhat reluctant to accept as she was longing for the reassuring feel of Gaetano's strong arms around her, but she acquiesced with grace. Over the man's shoulder, she watched as the alluring blonde cousin pulled Gaetano close. The two were laughing gaily and the woman was studying Gaetano's face as if she were going to attempt to paint it. When the song ended, Evelina hugged the groomsman and thanked him for a lovely dance and his profuse good wishes. She moved toward Gaetano and the clinging cousin. As she approached, Evelina observed her husband attempting to pull away from his attentive dance partner in a gentle and tactful way. Just as he wriggled free and turned toward Evelina, the woman reached up as if to pat Gaetano's face and then made a quick motion that was difficult for Evelina to follow. Gaetano's head jerked back and the cousin's arms fell to her sides. Evelina looked up at her groom to see minuscule drops of blood rising in a row across his cheek. *Had the woman scratched him?* Evelina nimbly placed herself in front of Gaetano and lifted his hand to her waist. She swayed to the rhythm of the lilting music. Her new husband caught on and the two of them danced away from the woman who lingered on the makeshift dance floor, her arms hanging limply beside her, an odd, vacant smile on her face.

The newly married couple did not discuss the cousin's actions. Evelina took the delicate cotton handkerchief her nonna had embroidered with blue flowers from inside her sleeve and wiped the scratch on Gaetano's face. The two finished their dance and held each other close as they danced again and again. Evelina noticed the cousin just once more while gliding around the polished floor with her groom. The peculiar woman was standing rigidly up against the white stone wall of the long hall, a little apart from some other of Gaetano's clan. Her face had gone entirely expressionless. She did not approach Evelina or Gaetano again that evening. "*La povera donna. She must be ill*," theorized the young bride.

The evening drifted along without further disturbance as Gaetano guided his ravishing new wife around and around the dance floor, whispering close to her ear. "Your magnificent dress is almost, though not quite fine enough for you, Darling. And the way your shining hair is done up without a single flaw is exquisite! I cannot wait to make a complete mess of it the minute we climb into our getaway car," he teased. Evelina let herself bask in Gaetano's attentiveness and take pleasure in the compliments he offered, as any bride would. She surrendered her anxieties about Saverio to Ennio's capable hands.

After their fourth or fifth dance in a row, Gaetano turned from Evelina and released his close embrace. With a spin and a flourish, he relinquished his wife to Ennio who had cut in on their waltz. Evelina had not seen the diminutive rector behind her husband's tall, athletic form until Gaetano stepped away. Now she reached out her arms to her dear friend with a warm smile. Ennio placed himself woodenly in Evelina's arms leaving plenty of space between them. Evelina did most of the leading as they tiptoed around the floor. Just as the two were getting into a bit of a rhythm with their steps, Ennio leaned in, stomping on the toes of Evelina's white satin pumps. During the ensuing pause, he said into the bride's ear, "My people tell me that Saverio has gone to the other side of the city. Your departing guests will be chaperoned, at any rate, so enjoy your special evening, mia cara."

"Your people, Ennio?" said Evelina raising the eyebrows that had, just this morning been shaped in neat arches for this momentous day.

"You do not believe that I have people, Evelina?" Ennio teased. "I'm what they call a 'big deal' in our fair city you know!"

For the first time in many days, Evelina laughed aloud at his words and crooked smile. She playfully mussed the unruly ebony hair of her friend and advocate even further as they picked up their awkward ballet.

Evelina genuinely enjoyed herself for the rest of the evening, confident in Ennio's reassurances. She and Gaetano danced with their guests, made toasts and were toasted, drank, and heartily ate. Anyone in attendance would have agreed that it was a wonderful, triumphant wedding reception, nothing other than the happiest of celebrations; and, for the most part, it was.

Even though they hadn't been successful in keeping Saverio away, the most important thing was that the wedding was accomplished. It had been well celebrated. Evelina belonged to Gaetano now, in a blessed, sacramental way and this offered her another kind of sanctuary.

She was grateful that not one person at the gathering approached her to ask about the stranger with the sallow skin and thick, titian hair. For once, Evelina was glad that vampyres possessed the ability to come and go unseen.

As the hour approached for the bride and groom to take leave of their guests, the two began giving last hugs and thanking each attendee for witnessing their ceremony. Evelina looked about for Gaetano's sad cousin. Unfortunately, amid the bustle and celebration, she couldn't find the fair young woman. *Perhaps I can pay her a visit when we get back. The roses at St. Catherine's will still be blooming. I'll take a bouquet,* she decided. Gaetano moved his bride toward the door of the hall, and to the waiting hired limousine that would take them to the airport for their flight to Paris.

Ennio appeared at Evelina's side just as the couple reached the long black car. A bit of wedding cake stuck to the corner of his mouth, he leaned to her ear and whispered. "Blessings on your marriage. Enjoy your holiday with your new husband and be concerned about no one else, my darling one."

Evelina smiled at Ennio and gave a grateful nod. Gaetano helped her into the back of the long car. He lifted her skirt in after her with great care before bounding around the back of the vehicle to the other side door. He leaped in and the car bounced up and down. Evelina laughed as she held her pearl-encrusted headpiece in place. And then, with a final wave to Ennio and blown kisses to their guests, the newlyweds were off.

CHAPTER 3
THE CLAIRVOYANCE

Crepuscular sarcophagi of the horde
Who scrape and scratch each others' bones
As an inglorious array of obscene animus
Bewitches the virginal seer.

E velina felt safe in Paris. She walked about without restriction or fear, even at night, with Gaetano by her side. She supposed her new husband would not necessarily be able to defend himself or keep her safe from a tenacious vampire. All the same, he *was* an imposing figure. Ennio had said many times that most of the undead preyed upon the weak. Her hope was that Gaetano's physical strength and confidence would be something of a deterrent at least.

Saverio was mentioned by name in more than one dusty, antiquated text that Ennio had found in the Vatican's not so secret library. Evelina knew that her vampiric stalker had been in Paris often during his centuries-long existence. He had hidden in the catacombs underneath the city and, presumably, roamed the Paris boulevards by night, stalking the innocent. The City of Light might not have been Evelina's first choice for a carefree getaway, but Gaetano considered Paris the most romantic of the world's cities and she could not disagree. A letter that arrived at their hotel on the second day of the couple's honeymoon stay had eased Evelina's worries about the vampire's Paris connection. In it, Ennio explained that he had been keeping close track of Saverio's movements since the wedding with the help of a half-dozen priests of his order – his "people", as it were. The note assured Evelina, again, that she could rest easily on her holiday safe in the knowledge that the chambers beneath Rome were Saverio's home and the venerable city above them, his haunt. Rarely an hour went by, assured Ennio, when one of those on alert to the monster's movements did not observe him there. Further, Ennio wrote, he would send a telegram if there were any unusual movements on Saverio's part.

Evelina so wished to be free to luxuriate in her temporary respite that she chose to believe Saverio was unaware of Ennio's spies and, therefore, would not bother to veil his movements from their eyes. *But he was right there at my wedding celebration.* She pushed the encroaching thought away.

Folding Ennio's reassuring letter into her sky-blue clutch, Evelina imagined Saverio stealing along the paths between the skeletons embedded in the caves underneath Rome. The clergyman, with the mysterious privilege he often enjoyed, had once given Evelina a private tour of the skull-lined walls below the great city. She had avoided Italy's catacombs throughout her young life, even when Masses were said there at certain times of the year. Ignoring her aversion to the dark recesses, her cohort suggested again and again that they explore the underground tombs and tunnels. Over time, Ennio's persistence wore her down and Evelina agreed to go exploring with him in hopes of putting an end to his nagging. The expedition turned out to be much shorter than planned. Within a breath of walking into the first chamber on their tour, Evelina stopped. Turning slowly in place, she found that she could see more than just bones; she could divine transparent visions of the faces and flesh that had once covered them. She was able to make out even the phantoms' facial expressions. Tears welled up in her eyes and then streamed down her face. Her body shook as she let out small mewling sobs: her own quiet keening. The tour was over, but Ennio was satisfied. His long-harbored suspicions about the dynamism of Evelina's empathic gifts were confirmed. Admitting to feeling a little guilty for tormenting his friend so, Ennio ushered the overwrought seer back to the entrance of the dark channels and out into the sunshine. He helped her to sit on the walkway and encouraged her to lower her head and take several deep breaths.

Ennio and Evelina had, together, studied parts of the reportedly cursed Grand Grimoire after their first encounter with Saverio. For safety's sake, they were not allowed access to the original text less formally known as the Red Dragon. But in an ornate study room of the Vatican, they pored over reproduced pages of the tome that had been blessed by a long-dead Pope and learned that vampyres must steer clear of the bones of saints. Relics of the pure had an even more disturbing effect on the undead than holy water, according to the medieval codex of the supernatural. They had always wondered how Saverio was able to use the catacombs to traverse a city during the daytime hours when he could not walk around above ground. After her disturbing excursion, Evelina realized that buried among the few innocent and holy below the city, were many more unrepentant sinners who had worn masks of virtue in life like a disguise.

An hour or so after their abbreviated outing, as they sipped fortifying espresso at an open-air cafe, Ennio explained to a recovered Evelina that God had gifted her with what modern scientists described as rapidly firing synapses in her brain. This made her unusually empathic. It was the reason she was able to pick up signals from even those who had died centuries ago. "A gift from God?" Evelina protested. "It felt much more like a curse in that horrible place." She often had long conversations with her dead parents: albeit, these talks happened in her dreams. There were also times when she would see a figure out of the corner of her eye in a graveyard. These specters faded away when she looked full upon them. Oh, but never had she sensed anything as vividly or seen anything as awful as she had in the catacombs. She hoped never to repeat the experience and made this quite clear to Ennio.

"Imagine that you had a cold heart toward the orphaned children in your charge? What if you could not love God's creations the way that you do?" Ennio had pressed as they discussed Evelina's abilities. "Do you not consider your capacity for love, care, and kindness a gift?"

Evelina had to admit that she did not wish to be like some of the heartless people with whom she had crossed paths. It would be awful to be a person who could exhibit cruelty to animals and God's human creations. She did not want to be able to look right through another and feel nothing. Still, she wondered how having empathy with even the long-dead could be considered a useful or positive thing.

This aspect of her brain's workings felt more like a disturbance of its synapses than an enhancement of them, assuming Ennio's theory about her cerebral activity held water. After some thought, she concluded that, like many things in life, her peculiarities were both a blessing and a curse.

And so, Evelina did not glimpse the predator she feared each day in Rome as she and Gaetano walked the Paris streets. She gave all of her attention to her new husband and the making of honeymoon memories and did not sense Saverio or any other of his kind. She relaxed in a way she hadn't done in many months. As the lovers strolled along the streets of the grand city, they linked arms, often with Evelina's head nestled cozily into Gaetano's shoulder. Throughout the halcyon days of their perfect holiday, the two traded whispered endearments and intimate caresses.

One afternoon, the enchanted twosome visited the Musée National d' Art. The director there was a man her parents had called Alain when they worked together during the war. His given name was Jean Cassou. The couple was able to speak with the busy man for a few minutes, and he offered them his warmest wishes for their union. Afterward, the two pretended to study the splendid pieces in the collections of the museum for several hours, though, to be sure, they had eyes only for each other.

Each day the contented pair dined in the warm sunshine and made plans for their long, shared future. In the evenings, they danced in the shadow of the Eiffel Tower and roamed the Avenue Des Champs-Élysées.

During the night, Evelina, shy, reserved schoolgirl that she had once been, gave herself to Gaetano in ways she had held in reserve during their courtship. Gaetano was a skilled, selfless lover with a slow and steady hand. Evelina delighted in his attentions. No visions of monsters or demons plagued her mind as warm breezes blew open the lacy white curtains of their room and she and her husband explored one another's bodies throughout each long honeymoon night.

As the satisfied lovers curled up together in the darkest hours of each morning, however, Saverio did materialize. He came to Evelina in her dreams, blighting the perfect requiescence of the days and evenings. As she slept she would feel pointed teeth on her throat and a preternaturally lean, muscular body pressed against her. At the instant she stopped struggling and began to anticipate the release of the vampire's kiss, her eyes would open to find Gaetano's warm, tall body spooned around her smaller figure. She would allow herself to indulge in a few moments of frustrated crying before settling in to calm her breathing. Once she had composed herself, she would awaken her husband with a touch and they would make fierce love until blessed daylight returned.

CHAPTER 4
THE PROPHECY

Malevolent warnings,
The destiny of the damned,
Emerge from a pall of lurid shadow,
Obsessions to excite.

On Saturday, one week after the grand wedding that Gaetano still did not know had been slightly tainted by the presence of an encroacher, Evelina and her unwary groom took the Metro to Vaneau station. They had a plan to search out the magnificent St. Vincent De Paul chapel. The two followed other worshipers and located the holy place they sought, concealed inside an unobtrusive building. The exterior looked very much like that of a business or residence. It stood, tucked between other similar buildings, with only its turquoise door and a simple, sand-colored cross atop the acroterion to distinguish it. Inside, the majesty of the chapel took away Evelina's breath. Gaetano, too, looked up at the elaborate decorations of the arched ceilings and inhaled deeply before he tucked Evelina's arm under his and the two started up the center aisle. He chose a pew and stepped aside to let Evelina lead the way.

Under the ornate blue and gold ceiling, seated on a gleaming wooden pew and nestled against a giant white marble column, the young couple participated in a vigil Mass. Afterward, they climbed the double staircase to view the body of St Vincent. Rather, they viewed his skeleton covered by a wax likeness of the man in repose. What Evelina felt in the presence of the ornamented relics was kindness personified. The couple said a special prayer for the poor in the city of Rome before the glass reliquary housing the remains of the generous Saint who, in life, had championed the destitute. They prayed that they would remember to serve the less fortunate each day of their shared lives. After their visit with the saint, husband and wife strolled through the surrounding, pleasant neighborhoods and chatted about Evelina's plans for the upcoming school year at the orphanage. She was not only a patron of the institution but whiled away a good many of her days there, teaching and guiding the children. Or, as some of the nuns affectionately claimed, spoiling them.

As the pair meandered about, they scouted for a romantic spot to eat the final evening meal of their honeymoon retreat. The morning would bring the three-hour flight back to Rome and the dawning of their day-to-day married life. It might not, Evelina supposed, be altogether normal but she hoped that it would be safe enough. When the pair came upon a wooden bench tucked up against the wall of another of the perpetual white stone edifices, Evelina sat to rest. In front of the building, a flower vendor hawked her wares. Gaetano captured an armful of white roses at the little flower stand and dug into his pants pocket for the francs with which to pay the vendor. Smiling at his wife, he placed the bouquet delicately in her arms. "Are your senses full of the perfume of your roses, mia amore, or do you also smell pastry?" he quipped with his nose lifted high, sniffing the air around them.

"I do smell it," Evelina laughed. "And it is making me more than a bit hungry!"

"Wait here. I will see if I can locate the goodies," the eager Gaetano suggested, rubbing his hands together. Without another word, he slipped down a cross street to follow the heavenly aroma that had wafted to them.

Night terrors aside, Evelina had not felt so loved and doted on in a long time. She closed her eyes and let the slight, warm breeze caress her face, neck, and arms, luxuriating in the feeling of freedom and safety. Every few seconds, she lifted the roses to her nose to breathe in their sweet scent. When several minutes had passed, she felt the weight of someone else ease on to the bench beside her. Thinking Gaetano had reappeared, she turned her head toward the movement. Smiling, she opened her eyes.

"Are you truly so happy to see me?" sneered Saverio.

Evelina tried to stand and the graceful white roses scattered at her feet. Even as she leaned forward to rise, Saverio grabbed her arm and jerked her back to the bench.

"Leave us alone, Saverio" Evelina exhorted, affecting more

confidence than she felt. She knew that her protests were useless. Her disappointment was so great that it overshadowed her alarm. She wasn't dreaming now; the devil had followed her to Paris and he meant to intrude upon her honeymoon as he had upon her wedding. As it was each time the beast invaded her life, she feared that this time he meant to do her, or her beloved, real harm.

Saverio's pale, cold face leaned over hers until Evelina was bent backward with her bare upper back almost touching the hard, wooden bench. Saverio's heavy, coppery hair fell to create a tent around her face. In spite of herself, Evelina drank in the scent of him. Though he frequented dank, musty places, Saverio always smelled of exotic spices.

"You know you belong to me. You will always be mine, Evelina," Saverio whispered as his riotous green eyes examined her face and to her horror, her neck. "Let me take you away from here."

His provocative words enabled Evelina to push down her fear and revulsion and respond. With all the command she could muster, she pronounced, "Never, you animal. I am not yours and will not ever be. My heart belongs to my husband, but I am no one's property. You saved my life once. I am grateful to you for not letting me be killed and, I suppose, for not killing me yourself. But, Saverio, hear me. Gratitude notwithstanding, you have no claim to me of any kind."

"I stake my claims where I will." Saverio gave a low, soft laugh. "If I say you are mine, you are mine. But I will not force you, mia amore."

Force her? A new wave of panic rushed over Evelina. Her heart raced uncontrollably, and her breath came in short gasps. Evelina managed to gasp her question, "Did you think I would choose to come away with you?"

Saverio reached up and gently tucked Evelina's hair behind her ear and she quivered at his touch. She took a deeper breath so she could speak aloud again. In defiance of her fear and intimidation, she asserted, "If Ennio were here, you would be dead already Saverio."

"Don't threaten me with your puny man of God," spat the demon. "I can manage that mosquito as I have managed many a pathetically sincere and determined priest over the centuries." He gave a short, derisive snort. "Ah, mia bellezza, I am not here to make you my own; not today. I come to you with a warning. You are facing a danger much worse than my ardent affections. Be vigilant. Take note of the cycle of the moon. I will be watching you." His face no longer registered amusement. His eyes searched Evelina's. She felt he was seeking a sign that she had heard and would heed his warnings. When he said that he would be watching her, it felt more like a promise than a threat.

Saverio continued to speak but in a lower tone. Evelina could not quite catch the words; was it something about strength and fortitude? She could lean back no further. Her vision spun and her heart raced faster still. A flush of fever ran through her body. As it reached her face, she eased into an almost hypnotic trance in which her breath came in short bursts, yet her limbs relaxed. As Saverio bent his lips to the vein in her neck, she gave in without dread and, turning her head, opened herself to him. She felt his lips on her burning skin and her pulse pounding in her carotid artery. Rather than the piercing bite Evelina anticipated, Saverio placed a light, lingering kiss on that spot. As he sat up, she could see that his teeth were white and even. They looked like those of an ordinary man. No razor-sharp canines could be seen at the corners of his petal pink lips. His green eyes held a look that seemed to his captive like one of care and concern, perhaps even tenderness.

Evelina fainted.

CHAPTER 5
THE INCUBUS

An ominous shadow of deadly fright
Sickens and stabs one vanquished heart.
It boils and buries pristine delusions
In a cauldron of despair.

Evelina awakened back in her austere, yet comfortable hotel room lying on the bed. Her shoes were off, and her lavender dress was folded neatly over the arm of the nearby, sage green, upholstered chair. Gaetano sat on the edge of the chair, watching her. A crisp white sheet and matelaisé coverlet had been tucked around her up to her shoulders. Evelina's soft, sleepy brown eyes opened, and Gaetano shifted over to sit beside his wife on the bed.

"Gaetano," Evelina questioned. "How did I get here?"

"I carried you here, mia tesora," he answered.

"Oh, yes, I do remember now, being in your arms." Images

of the hours since the interaction with Saverio and her resultant fainting spell were presenting themselves to Evelina's fogged mind. "No, not all that way?" she enjoined, "All that way from the bench? Without taking the Metro?"

"Yes. It was no great task for me. The important question is, are you well, Darling? What happened to you?" Gaetano's countenance revealed a great degree of concern.

"I just became a bit dizzy. Maybe it was hunger." Evelina, of course, knew the true reason for her spell.

"A bit dizzy? You have been in and out of consciousness for more than an hour, my darling. When we return to Rome tomorrow, you must see a doctor. That is if you are well enough by morning to fly home. If you do not make a spirited recovery, we will find a doctor here in Paris." Gaetano stood and gave a brusque swipe to Evelina's already smooth and tidy covers. He announced, "But for now, yes, my love, you must eat."

Gaetano had seen to it that dinner be brought to the room. When Evelina saw the beef on the plate sitting in its red juices, she grew weak once again. She was able to eat some bread and drink the sweet, burgundy-colored wine that Gaetano poured for her. Afterward, her new husband produced a white box tied with a blue ribbon. In it were a half dozen Charlotte aux framboises. They were a bit worse for wear; still, Gaetano had somehow managed to carry them, along with his wife, back to the hotel and she was grateful for it. Evelina ate two and felt her strength returning bit by bit. She still felt tired and disoriented, but she convinced Gaetano that no doctor would be needed that evening.

There was no newlywed lovemaking on their last night in Paris. Gaetano's sleep was restless. Evelina believed he must have been dreaming throughout the nighttime hours. He made low grunting noises as he tossed around in the bed. He sounded a bit like a puppy growling as it played with a new toy. Evelina, unable to sleep, meditated on Saverio's words. As much as she wished she could put it out of her mind, she recalled, too, Saverio's kiss. It was never wise, she ruminated, to not pay attention when Saverio spoke. He had such power, and she never knew when it might be used for ill. Forewarned is forearmed, she decided. She used this as an excuse to contemplate the action of Saverio's icy lips on her neck just above the string of her mother's pearls that she often wore. He had placed those bloodless lips right against the place where her carotid artery thrummed near the surface of her smooth skin. Evelina assumed this would be the vein a vampyre would penetrate with his pointed fangs if he meant to drain a victim's blood with proficiency. The idea made her quake with a fever-like chill.

That kiss, she pondered, it was not the type one would expect from a blood-sucking creature of the night; not at all. It was a gentle, almost delicate kiss. It was not demanding or cruel. Saverio, she knew, was not capable of devotion, only offense. Why would a vicious knave, such as he must be, protect her? To preserve her for himself? Was he saving her for some horrible plan he had fashioned? She imagined he might implement his terrible scheme when he had grown tired of teasing her, like a mighty jungle cat with a tiny mouse. *And I thanked him for it.* She was annoyed by her recent artlessness.

She could not imagine a danger worse than that of being turned into a soulless immortal. This was her greatest fear with regard to Saverio's oppressions. Saverio had said he would not force her. Force her to do what? And one couldn't believe him. What was a lie in the face of the carnage Saverio had generated through the ages? These were questions Evelina had asked herself countless times throughout the past few years. Now she wondered too, what the moon could have to do with some impending danger. The moon held no sway over vampyres as far as she knew. She'd never read of such a possibility, nor had Ennio ever mentioned it. Evelina shivered in the warm June night and tugged a small part of the coverlet that Gaetano had twisted about in his restless sleep up around her chin.

She longed to go home to confer with her patron and confidant. The honeymoon and Paris were no longer the sanctuary or holiday that Evelina had been savoring. She knew she would not find another carefree moment to enjoy Paris with her new husband, knowing that Saverio was lurking about. She would be on the plane home tomorrow even if Gaetano had to carry her aboard as he had carried her to this room.

Ennio would have insights for her. She needed, once more, for him to explain the power of the vampyre, especially strong in one as ancient as Saverio, to mesmerize and control. She needed to hear her priest's comforting words to assuage the guilt she felt for the desire Saverio's delicate, sweet kiss had aroused in her. She craved absolution for her sinful musings.

CHAPTER 6
THE THEURGY

Clairvoyant children of mystical parentage
Cast out thick cobwebs and obscuring clouds.
Bodies trapped within the viscous slime of perversion
Are at last exhumed.

For all the impatience she had felt on her last night in Paris to meet with him, Evelina put off a visit to Ennio for more than two weeks after she and Gaetano returned from their sojourn. She was still anxious to talk with her priest about the night Saverio had accosted her on the rough Paris bench. Her procrastination stemmed from the fact that other matters were surfacing between she and her new husband that she did not look forward to sharing with her pastor. All the same, she knew in her heart that she would have to address these concerns before long. As uncomfortable as it might be, the nervous bride had decided that today she would lay out all of her worries for Ennio's inspection.

"Now what do you want to confess to the good Father about this honeymoon of yours, mia cara," wisecracked Ennio as he and Evelina eased themselves into two indigo leather chairs across from each other. They each held a dainty white teacup and saucer edged in Wedgwood blue that had been given to the rectory by some wealthy parishioner a century ago.

"Don't be smart. And, for goodness sake, don't be vulgar, Ennio. You sound like every other man in the world or, at least, like the common ones."

"I am very much like every other man in the world, little one. We are all common," replied Ennio with a crooked smile. His black hair stuck up in tufts around his face, accentuating his dancing blue eyes. Evelina thought to herself with a smile that no one would consider Ennio common in any way. Without a doubt, he did not look like "every other man." His face was gentler, his eyes kinder and more caring. And there was no mistaking that his ever-present Roman collar marked him as one who was not supposed to make lewd references, even in the company of his oldest friend.

The two of them had known each other since their grade school play-yard days. Back then, Ennio had held funeral services for the tiny dead birds and rodents that Evelina would find in the copse of trees that lined the church and school gardens. The young girl would come to her playmate with the small mouse or bird wrapped in her handkerchief. Tears would be pouring down her face. Ennio would help her find a proper burial place and bless the ground. Saying comforting words about the kindness of the

Lord, the future man of the cloth would cover the poor, wee varmint with earth he had dug with his small child hands. After the "services," Ennio would dry his friend's tears with his own handkerchief. Evelina smiled again as she remembered those days and her dear mother on laundry day always wondering how her daughter could lose so many hankies.

Ennio had been the guardian of Evelina's sensitive, caring nature for many years. Evelina's parents had been active members of the allied resistance during the war. When they lost their lives in the crash of a small plane near the war's end, a crash that may or may not have been an accident, Evelina was still in her early teens. Ennio's efforts to protect Evelina became more uncompromising after her tragic loss. He cared for her without apology and grew even more protective than he had been during the first years of the war when Rome was being bombed at random intervals.

Ennio's memory of his own mother's kind eyes and loving embrace was distant and dim. He did not recall if any father had been present in his early life, nor did he know what had become of the black-haired mother of his vague memories. He had grown up in the orphanage run by the Sisters of Mercy; the very community where Evelina would one day give of her time and resources. The nuns there answered his questions about his parentage with "I don't know" or "it was before my time".

The Sisters of St. Catherine's adored Ennio. Few of their charges went into seminary and even fewer came out as priests of the holy church. But Ennio had always been special to his caregivers and he returned the warm feelings of the nuns. As he often said, he did not have a mother; he had many. There were even some among his many mothers who had encouraged the gifts he had displayed as a child.

When the nuns were ill, his prayers for them were fervent and almost always answered. The good sisters noticed, when he was quite young, that he had a certain intuition about people, their characters, and their motives.

When Ennio was just seven years old, a nattily-dressed, sincere, and amiable man came to the orphanage. The man asked Mother Superior for permission to visit his dear niece. The man named one of the youngest of the little girls in the care of the nuns. Ennio happened to be studying a school worksheet at a long table along with several other boys, all under the watch of Sister Rosa Maria. When Ennio related the incident to Evelina later, he said that he had known the man was bad. When Evelina asked how he knew, he couldn't explain in any concrete way. He said that he supposed God had told him. Evelina understood.

The man persisted with his request in a charming, convincing manner. Mother Angelica was smiling as she began to look around for a sister who was not too busy to go and fetch the girl the man claimed as his niece. Ennio stood and walked away from the table of boys. He was an obedient child, but on this day he ignored Sister Rosa when she called him back. He strode with purpose up to Mother Superior and the well-dressed man. Little Ennio looked up at the man and challenged him. "You are wicked." Get out of here," he commanded. Mother Angelica gasped. She tried to shoo Ennio back toward sister Rosa who was hurrying over to retrieve her charge. Ennio stood his ground. He shouted at the man who had not moved but was looking decidedly uncomfortable, "Get out! In the name of God, get out!"

As Sister Rosa reached Ennio and guided him by his thin shoulders away from the shaken man and Mother Angelica, who was apologizing for Ennio's behavior, Ennio turned his head to maintain eye contact with the "bad man". Something in the glare of the small boy must have convinced the man it was time to go because he made a hasty retreat, calling back to Mother Superior that he would come back at a better time.

It was just a few days later when Ennio reported to Evelina that he had been called to Mother Angelica's office. Mother Angie asked him, just as Evelina had, how he had known the man was wicked. Ennio gave her the same answer he had given his friend; he just knew. Mother told him that he had, indeed, been right. "The man you confronted was not a relative of any of the children, Ennio. Did you know this?" Ennio admitted that he did know it. When Mother persisted in her inquiry asking how in the world Ennio could have known about the man, Ennio told her that he could see the man's ugly soul. Mother interrogated him no more.

While the kind nun did not bring up the subject of the contemptible man again, she called upon young Ennio often to help look after the smallest children, or to sit with those who were not well. Almost everyone in the orphanage, the school, the church, and the parish knew there was something extraordinary about the boy who asked for little and gave much. As a consequence, when Evelina's parents would request that Ennio be allowed to accompany them on a family outing, permission would be granted. Evelina's mother and father doted on Ennio and encouraged the relationship between the two young people. Ennio was devastated by the catastrophe that took the two treasured people from his life as well as Evelina's. The two teens became even closer as they worked through their mutual grief.

Defying the wishes, orders, and efforts of the Brothers in charge of Ennio's higher education, he and Evelina remained inseparable even during the years he studied in seminary. The pair enjoyed a familiarity born of shared experience and loss. They considered their relationship exempt from seminary rules on the grounds that they were childhood soul mates and needed each other. While it likely did not hurt that Rome was preoccupied with the establishment of a new Italian government and the church was busy trying to reconcile, or as Ennio said, excuse its wartime actions in those turbulent days, Evelina and Ennio got away with their association for the most part because the seminary Brothers knew what they had in Ennio. The anchorites were under orders, from much higher above, to routinely object and issue warnings. They had been further instructed, however, not to take any real action that might drive Ennio away from his studies. Word of his potential as a warrior for the forces of good had made it to the highest levels of the Vatican when Ennio was still in pre-seminary classes. After his unique talents were noted in the classroom and, of course, by the powerful Mother Angelica, he had been followed for years by agents of the Holy See. The hierarchy was aware of his aptitude for seeking out and negating human evil. They hoped this gift would extend to malevolent spiritual forces. Ennio was destined for a particular and sensitive role within the church.

Ennio knew that the church had plans for him. He also knew something that his superiors did not; that Evelina, in addition to her loving nature, had an intuitive prowess that would help him in his life's work. All that Evelina knew about her maternal grandmother, Nonna Alessandra's abilities was that she oftentimes saw things in her dreams that later came true. Ennio tried to tell his cohort that he had learned, from Vatican texts, that there was much more to her ancestry than intuitive dreaming. Evelina teased that he knew too much altogether. With a broad smile, she needled, "Are you saying that I am a witch, Ennio?"

"The very whitest of witches, perhaps, my friend," Ennio had replied with one of his crooked smiles.

For better or worse, Ennio's attempts to introduce Evelina to a power in which she had little interest were for naught. Even her ordeal in the skull-lined passageways had not swayed her. She remained innocence itself. She was always and ever so loving that no cruel, bitter nun (and there were a few of those who taught Evelina through the years), or even a soulless ghoul that stalked the innocent was too mean or lowly to enjoy her mercy, forgiveness, or help. Ennio believed that the gentle young woman needed someone with a cooler head and harder heart to be her defender. He had charged himself with the job on their first day of school together, as he had confessed to Evelina some years later. That first day, he witnessed Evelina smile beatifically at Sister Mary Monica and try to hug the pernicious nun after the "good Sister" had torn a delightful drawing of a dog Evelina had done from the girl's notebook and crumpled it in a fit of pique for reasons unknown. Some of Evelina's classmates believed her naïve or weak. The truth was that she was not naïve, but unspoiled, not weak, but filled with hope.

Yet, no matter their history, Evelina couldn't let her cherished friend get away with his naughty remarks about her honeymoon. This was the game they played, the dynamic they cultivated because it worked for them. She was the innocent young thing, he the good Father.

She sampled her tea and replaced her cup in its saucer. "He came to me in Paris," she announced. Ennio stopped, poised to sip. Evelina proceeded to tell him everything. At least she told him nearly everything.

CHAPTER 7
THE DIVINATION

Necromancers of morbid wickedness,
Synonymously Lucifer's adversaries,
Machinate and scheme without art,
Unleashing foul monstrosities.

W hen she had finished her report of Saverio's assault upon her in the City of Light, Ennio rubbed his hand over his face and let out a heavy sigh. He leaned toward Evelina and held her eyes with his as he spoke with profound seriousness. It was clear that he meant to make himself understood. "What you *must* remember, mia cara, is that Saverio is in no way capable of any kindness or caring act. He is a soulless demon who cannot experience human sentiment. He cannot love. He is a savage beast. He lives by the instinct to hunt, always. He has grown cunning through centuries of tracking and oppressing his victims. This you must always and ever keep foremost in your mind. I know that he has a power that is difficult to resist. It is a part of his nature and the venom he uses to stun his prey before the kill."

"Nonetheless, Ennio, he hasn't killed me," protested Evelina.

Ennio leaned farther forward, taking Evelina's hands in his. "Not yet, my dear one, not yet he hasn't." He paused as he searched Evelina's face. She knew he wanted her to acknowledge that Saverio was pure evil. She knew Ennio wanted her to believe that Saverio had stalked her for years with the intent to, one day, kill her, or, worse, turn her. Still, she could not forget the look in Saverio's eyes in Paris, the expression that wasn't mocking or obscene. It was a look that had made her feel he was worried for her.

Ennio lifted Evelina's hands and gave them a shake. "Please listen to me, Evelina," he went on. "Saverio possesses a supernatural gift for deception. It is not surprising that he is able to draw you in and play on your sympathies. I know that no matter how doggedly I insist that you must resist his charms, you may be unable to. Though you possess a strong will, your sympathy for others is stronger. Therefore, it is my job to protect you from Saverio's vile poison. I intend to do just that. You know that I have pledged to do so." He paused a few seconds before he continued. "My determination aside, mia cara, you are now a married woman who will continue to travel with her husband. You may one day leave Rome behind and move to some distant place where I cannot follow but Saverio surely will. Evelina, perhaps it is time to tell Gaetano about your unholy suitor."

"No, that isn't possible," Evelina protested. She pulled back, removing her hands from Ennio's. "Gaetano wouldn't understand; he couldn't. This whole business is too much for *anyone* to comprehend. You and I have been living it. Isn't it almost too much for you to grasp? It is for me! Furthermore, I am never leaving Rome or you. I can't believe that you even suggested it." Evelina was indignant and fully aware that her jaw was clenched, with her bottom lip poked out in a resolute pout.

"Yes, I do understand what you are saying, Evelina, but we must think of your safety. We need Gaetano's help," Ennio urged. "It has become evident that a union blessed by the Holy Church means nothing to Saverio. We once had hopes that the sacrament of marriage would afford you some added protection from Saverio's advances. I think we can discard that notion now. I sent you off to Paris thinking that you would be safe; that I had sheltered you with my hollow blessings and pathetically fallible spies. I know now that I cannot protect you from afar. And Gaetano's ignorance makes him extremely vulnerable."

Ennio paused, but Evelina did not react or speak. He tried another tack. "Suppose, Evelina, that Gaetano is offered a grand promotion in another city?"

"I'll tell him if, and when that happens." Evelina was resolved.

"Well, suppose someone in Gaetano's family became ill? Don't try to tell me you wouldn't rush right to the side of that person to stay as long as you were needed."

"It is Gaetano that isn't well, Ennio," Evelina blurted. "I don't know what is the matter. He doesn't sleep. He eats the most awful rare meat and almost nothing else. I'm afraid for him." She concentrated on the faded indigo carpet as she spoke. She knew that, by her failure to meet his eyes, Ennio would realize that there was more to the story.

After a sharp intake of air at this disclosure, Ennio, always able to read between Evelina's lines, prompted, "Has he done any harm to you, mia piccola?"

Evelina studied the floor, stalling. When she answered her words were barely audible. "No, not in any real way. He hasn't meant to."

"Tell me now," thundered Ennio, half standing.

Evelina looked up. "Calm yourself, Ennio, it is nothing," she motioned for Ennio to sit. When he perched himself just on the edge of his chair, she continued in an almost pleading voice, "It is just that he is restless when he does close his eyes. He has, once or twice, clawed at me in his sleep and, well," she trailed off.

"What is it, Evelina? You must tell me all that you are able to so that I can help you," encouraged Ennio in a quieter voice, recovering his trademark sangfroid.

"Well," Evelina's words were hesitant and halting, "it is just that Gaetano has become angry. He has developed a churlishness that I have never seen in him before. He, well, he has just become a bit rough with his affections."

Ennio's eyes filled with tears he would not allow to spill out at this distressing news but he did not avert his gaze from Evelina's. He conveyed his empathy and love for the dismayed woman through his unwavering attention.

Evelina hesitated and then almost whispered, "He isn't my gentle bear of a man anymore, Ennio. Something is desperately wrong."

The holy man again took his friend's hand and sing-songed as to a child. "Shush, shush, mia cara. We will fix it. All will be well." He smiled at Evelina and patted the hand he held with his free one. Evelina's shoulders lowered bit by bit. She reclined back into the cozy chair. When she did, Ennio sat back as well. He became pensive. "He hasn't seen a doctor?" he quizzed.

"Oh, no," scoffed Evelina. "He becomes quarrelsome if I even mention a doctor. Gaetano doesn't seem to recognize that something is wrong. He insists that he feels better than he ever has. He says that marriage has made him 'a new man.'" She looked at her hands in her lap. "I fear he is right."

Ennio interviewed Evelina further about Gaetano's behavior since the wedding. She answered each inquiry as best she could though she considered many of his questions irrelevant, even silly. The examination went on for what seemed like hours to Evelina. At last, Ennio sat back in his chair with another great sigh.

"I don't know what all this means. I must think," he pondered. "Saverio said the moon? The moon," he trailed off. "Well, it is easier to see a vampyre approach in the moonlight." Evelina raised her eyes and watched his face as she often did while Ennio ruminated on a problem and processed his thoughts. He rubbed his hand over his face once, then again. Just as Evelina was deciding that she could wait no longer, the earnest cleric stood and walked to a bookshelf on the other side of his study. He bent to one knee as if genuflecting at the altar and pulled a thick volume from a low shelf. He stood, leafing page by page through the dusty, elderly looking text that was bound with faded green leather. Endless minutes later, he returned to his chair. His eyes remained fixed on the open pages.

"What is it, Ennio?" Evelina coaxed in a subdued tone.

She didn't want to break his focus but was unable to be patient with his private reflection any longer.

Ennio looked up from the book. He stared ahead not seeking Evelina's eyes. His face no longer displayed the look of studied concentration that was so familiar to Evelina. His look registered shock and fear. Evelina could see his chest lifting in a too fast cadence.

"My God, what is it, Ennio? Are you unwell?" He did not answer her. "Ennio, talk to me, please." Evelina left her chair to kneel at Ennio's feet and look up at his face. "Ennio!" she almost shouted.

Ennio shook his head from side to side. "Evelina, I believe your beloved has been corrupted."

"What are you talking about, Ennio? Corrupted how, and by what? Gaetano is not a vampyre. Don't you think I've learned enough about that awful subject to be able to tell if Saverio had attacked my husband?"

Ennio stared into space. He shook his head slowly side to side.

Evelina was pleading with him now, "Please, Ennio, please talk to me." She grabbed Ennio's shoulders and gave them a rough shake. "What *is* it," she cried with a sob. She felt Ennio was looking right through her. She shook him again. Drawing herself up, she ordered, "Look at me Ennio!" She affected her most imposing tone, the one she seldom used. On the rare occasions that she did, Ennio called it her Sister Evelina voice.

Ennio blinked several times in quick succession and then met the troubled woman's eyes. He started to move his lips. No sound came out. Evelina gave him one more shake. Ennio cleared his throat and at long last spoke. "Mia piccola, mia carissima Evelina. The moon; Saverio said to watch the moon.

There has been no full moon since your wedding. It will rise full in just a few days. Saverio has been watching you and Gaetano. He has been close to you both. He has learned something. He has smelled it."

"No, Ennio, no," Evelina whimpered through her tears. Her confidence and authority were gone now.

"Gaetano has been corrupted by the claw of the wolf. When the moon rises full in two days, he will *become* the wolf. Each symptom you've described tells me it will be so." He held the dusty volume out to her. She saw a drawing of a hideous being neither human nor animal, yet both. It appeared to be a deformed dog with a long snout and canine teeth far too large to fit any man's mouth. That being so, the thing with a canine's aspect stood on legs with long quadriceps and upright hips, taller than any dog or wild animal.

"No, Ennio," Evelina almost screamed. "There is no werewolf. There is no such thing, no, no," she sobbed. Lamentably, Evelina knew first hand that entities that presented as human hunted and killed. She knew that these beings carried within them triggers handed down through the ages that controlled their actions. Ancient alchemies imbued them with animal instincts that made them as dangerous as any wild beast. A morbid picture popped unbidden into her mind. She remembered her wedding dance and the blonde cousin with the lethal fingernails. Evelina's heart broke with the dawning realization that Ennio's conclusion was almost certainly correct.

CHAPTER 8
THE HAUNTING

Preternatural stalker lurking near;
A ghostly, ghoulish shade
That tracks footsteps of dread
To the verge of panicked screams
Before it dissipates to air.

The heartbroken, weary companions sat in silence. Tears coursed down Evelina's face. After a long minute or two, Ennio, ever in tune to Evelina's needs, pulled his handkerchief from the pocket of his vicar's black shirt. He knelt on the floor in front of Evelina, took her hand, and pressed the square of fabric into her palm in a familiar gesture. It comforted them both. Evelina looked up and summoned a sad smile for her oldest friend. Without words, Ennio stood and passed through the half-open pocket doors. Evelina heard his footsteps retreat and understood that he had gone to make more tea for them; tea with perhaps a splash of something more fortifying.

She was trembling and would welcome Ennio's brew. She thought about her dear Gaetano. A memory flashed through her mind of the day, two years ago, that the two had met. They had been in the church right next door. Evelina had turned to offer her hand in peace to the person with the resonant singing voice sitting behind her during that Sunday's service. It had been Gaetano and when their hands touched she had felt a charge of energy that tingled up her arm in a remarkably pleasing way. Gaetano had moved into the parish just a few weeks before and begun attending Ennio's Masses. From smiles and eye contact during subsequent Masses to longer and longer greetings during the sign of peace, and later to coffee afterward, she had found him uncommonly interesting and oh so attractive. He was outgoing, full of fun and had no awareness of, or anxiety about, monsters or devils. Evelina saw in him normalcy, security, a chance for happiness, and perhaps children of her own one day; which was her fondest wish. He had a kind heart, helping her to buy and wrap gifts and fill grocery baskets at Christmastime for the children living at the orphanage and the Sisters who cared for them. He was devout. He did not miss Mass on Sunday or Holy Days of obligation. Even so, he could fill a Saturday night with fun and harmless mischief and have Evelina laughing until tears rolled down her cheeks over his bawdiest and most outrageous stories. Gaetano grew ever more desirable as Evelina knew him better and better. His kisses were sometimes soft and sweet and often deliciously searching and arousing. His wit and magnetism were irresistible to

Evelina. With Gaetano in it, her life had taken on a glow that even her fear of Saverio's next intrusion could not diminish.

Now, though, her genial, devoted new husband was changed. They had lived just hours as husband and wife before something nefarious had come into their lives and laid waste to Evelina's hopes for a normal life. It was almost too much to bear. Evelina's instincts were, as ever, to comfort; to do whatever she could to improve the situation and help the helpless. As the empath she was, she felt the pain and suffering of her fellow humans and all God's creatures as keenly as if their heartaches were her own. But this was her Gaetano. He had been *her* deliverance. Days spent with him were more untroubled, more convivial than anything else that had ever afforded her relief from feelings of sadness. She had felt as deep a sense of loss and bewilderment just once before. Her world had crumbled on the day she was told of her parents' accident. It was unthinkable that the new life she had built for herself over the years since was dissolving around her.

Evelina did her best to fix her attention on the immediate problem at hand. She and Ennio must save her beloved. She tried to prepare herself to hear the worst and to do whatever it would take to return Gaetano to his old self. Ennio returned with two saucers and large, solid white mugs of brandy-laced tea. He handed one to Evelina and settled back into his chair as he blew on the other. They sipped in silence. Their shaking hands gradually became steadier as their breathing slowed to near normal rhythms. Evelina excused herself to the rectory powder room. When she returned, with eyes dry and hair freshly brushed, she sat back down and looked into her dearly loved companion's sad, blue eyes. "So," she said, to let him know she was ready to move forward.

To begin with, Ennio made it clear to Evelina that there was no one they could turn to for assistance. Ennio was the go-to man in the Vatican for this kind of thing, if there could be such a figure. Anyone who might have been characterized as a mentor to him was gone or no longer had the physical strength to help in a material way. One or two aged clerics prevailed in Rome who had been fighting evil manifest for decades. They could perhaps be consulted. But, other than the possibility of the advice and prayers of these sages, it would be up to the two young people to defend others from attack by the wild thing Gaetano would become. Just as importantly to Evelina, they would need to protect Gaetano himself as he transformed into a dangerous beast. To make matters worse, there was very little time for them to devise and execute a plan of action. The unfathomable metamorphosis would be happening in what was, in effect, just hours.

Evelina was quite sure that her poor husband had no idea what was happening to him. The first decision she and Ennio must make was whether they should try to explain all to Gaetano. Did they even have enough hours, wondered Evelina, and how could they possibly convince him? After much deliberation, they concluded that they must try. Gaetano would have to be contained in some way, according to the musty text from Ennio's shelf. He would need to be locked up during the hours the full moon could be seen in the sky above the city. This, of course, could be accomplished much more easily with his cooperation.

Evelina invited Ennio to come that evening to the

apartment she had been left by her parents and now shared with her husband. They would tell Gaetano all that they knew and pray that he could somehow understand. They would pray, too, that their frightening, unbelievable narrative would not cause Gaetano to run from them, making him impossible to restrain. As indicated by his recent agitation and aggressive behaviors, there was also the chance that he could become violent. Evelina feared that Ennio would come to her home armed against that possibility.

"You must promise me, Ennio, that you will not harm Gaetano," she implored him as he held the door open for her departure.

"Evelina, you know that I will do what I must to protect you. You are afraid that I will bring a weapon; a gun. I will not. I don't believe that kind of instrument will be necessary to subdue Gaetano tonight. Go home. Prepare yourself. Try to remain as calm as possible. I will be with you soon. I will arrive well before Gaetano is expected home so that we can talk."

Evelina was reassured by Ennio's words to some extent. She believed that he meant to protect both she and her beloved husband as they searched for the solution to this new horror that had invaded their lives. She took her compact red umbrella from her matching bag and opened it for protection against the intermittent rain showers of the gloomy morning. The gay accessories were jarringly out of sync with the dysphoria of the day. Evelina recalled the pleasurable morning of shopping for her honeymoon when she had made what was, for her, a frivolous purchase of the bright adornments. Today she wished she'd bought the black bag. What had she been thinking? Why would she make herself so conspicuous, so easy for Saverio to pick out of a crowd? *The color of blood; how foolish*, she chastised herself as she emitted a humorless titter. But then, she had no idea if vampyres even saw color as humans did. Perhaps their entire existence was to them like an old American horror movie one might find on television late of a Saturday evening.

She embarked on the short walk to the cozy upstairs flat where she had resided for most of her life. Gaetano had resided in a much more modern building when they met, but Evelina could not give up the place that held the memories of life with her famiglia di nascita. There was a bit of inheritance in addition to the apartment, the greater part of which had been used to support St. Monica's orphanage. Even though Evelina's generosity was considerable and ongoing, Gaetano's work at the bank and the simple life they led kept them comfortable. Another advantage of living in the old building was that it was close to Ennio's church. While she planned to have her strong, attentive husband by her side, Evelina felt she also needed the protector who knew of more dangers than Gaetano could dream. Having Ennio nearby made her feel safe, and Gaetano had never seemed to mind. Gaetano's warm personality had ensured that he and Ennio had become almost instant friends. While the relationship between Evelina and Gaetano had developed organically, or with God's help perhaps, and not by Ennio's design, he had certainly never objected.

Evelina hiked steadily onward toward the haven of her home. Her heels clicked on the damp pavement in a way that irritated her. She was flustered and nervy and the hollow sound heightened her anxiety with each step. The stone buildings that seemed so warm and inviting in the sunshine

49

exuded a sinister ambiance darkened and dripping with the drizzle of the misty, overcast day. The apprehensive young bride increased her pace as she turned the corner from the rectory. A tingling feeling squirmed its way up her spine as she ascended the hill to her building on the next street. The fine hairs on the back of her neck stood on end. Her heart hammered as she walked faster still. If she was correct in thinking Saverio was about, she knew an accelerated pace wouldn't help. He could move as mist and blend right into the surrounding fog to overtake her at any speed. Evelina realized that on a dark day like this one he could move about at will. He need not fear being burned by the sun's rays even had he not recently fed. She whipped her head from one side to the other and back again. She halted her pilgrimage three separate times and turned full circle to check behind her. She saw nothing unusual. When she reached the steps of the old stone building that housed her rooms, she caught a glimpse of a figure in black slipping around the corner away from the house. It could just as easily have been her imagination as a stalking fiend she told herself. Even so, she hurried inside and locked her door. Saverio had never been invited into her flat, and it was true that a vampyre could not enter a private home without an invitation. She would be safe within these walls, at least until her husband arrived.

CHAPTER 9
THE CHRONICLE

A mocking clock clangs without mercy
Each second a bloodthirsty assault.
Sixty tolls before the larger hand convulses into place.
Another unlovely death.

S hortly after three o'clock that afternoon, the bell
chimed at Evelina's home causing her to start. She had
alternated pacing with sitting burrowed in her favorite
overstuffed chintz-covered chair. It was splashed with joyful
pink cabbage roses in a way that was at complete odds with all
she was feeling on this harrowing day. All the while she had
roamed about the comfortable rooms or sat curled in the
chair, she had been thinking.

She went to the door, straightening the skirt of her lemon-
colored summer dress. She realized it must be Ennio who had
rung. This expectation aside, she checked by opening the
door a mere crack, leaving the security chain fastened. When

she saw that it was, indeed, her accomplice, she let him in. They embraced at once. It was an unusual greeting for them now that they were adults and Ennio was a parish priest. Today it felt appropriate, almost involuntary. When they dropped arms, they stood for a short while chatting about matters that would not seem important to an outside listener. Clouds and rainy weather had a vastly different meaning in their lives than they did for, say, vineyard workers.

After choosing tea over Evelina's coffee invitation, Ennio excused himself to freshen up. Evelina put on the kettle. When Ennio returned to the open living area where Evelina was pouring Earl Grey into large blue mugs, he said, "Evelina, we had better discuss what we will say to Gaetano when he arrives."

Evelina sighed and plunged in. "I've pondered this all day, Ennio. I have come around to your way of thinking. You are right. We must tell Gaetano all that has happened since our first meeting with Saverio. As it is now, Gaetano has no concept of such things, no frame of reference at all. He has been until this poison invaded his system, a fun-loving, hard-working, almost naive young man. He has known love, success, and happiness, but never before has he felt the touch of the damned as you and I have. I feel that there is just one way that he can come to an understanding of what is happening to him; a diplomatic introduction to the idea that monstrous, inhuman evil walks the earth in somatic form. Saverio's existence offers the most convincing proof of such things." With a short, dry laugh, and a complete reversal of the morning's attitude wrought by her husband's misfortune, she added, "Perhaps we should invite Saverio over to help us teach Gaetano about monsters."

"That is a staggeringly bad idea, my Darling," said Ennio. "Issuing an invitation to Saverio can help solve no problem." They both knew this quite well, of course. Ennio sighed heavily as he confirmed, "Still, you have perfectly expressed my own conclusions, mia cara. While a..."Ennio cleared his throat before continuing, "...demonstration is out of the question, I too believe the best way to proceed is to tell Gaetano of our adventures, if one may characterize the horror we have lived as such. He should have no reason to think we would lie to him." The two old friends looked into each other's eyes. Evelina found a sad disquiet in those of the padre that she knew was reflected in her own. This time they sighed in unison. There was nothing to do but move forward.

CHAPTER 10
THE SLAUGHTER

Bone-rattling tales of innocence wrecked,
Distant screams of horror,
As a clutch of gypsy beasts
Inflict necrosis with awful efficiency.

The two sat turned toward each other on the sofa in the apartment's cozy parlor; Evelina with one leg tucked underneath her, both with teacups in hand. They recapped the history and chronology of their association with Saverio, taking turns remembering important details. They did their best to organize their memoir to make it concise, clear, and they hoped, believable for Gaetano.

It had all begun almost five years ago when Evelina was in her first year of università at St Benedict's Accademia. Ennio had yet to take his final sacramental vows. That summer, he had been assigned to study in Vatican City and was now a brilliant young star of the seminary. His interest in, and knowledge of all things paranormal was out in the open among the Vatican curia. He was being groomed for the highly specialized, clandestine role of an exorcist. He knew there would be demons to face in his life and career but while he had read much about the myth of the vampyre, Ennio had never been certain of the existence of beings like Saverio.

One late May afternoon, after much study of things unholy and disturbing, Ennio called Evelina's dormitory at St Benedict's. He reached Sister Maria Leonetta and, as he told Evelina later, asked if he might speak to one of her students, Miss Delle Grazie. Identifying himself as *Father* Christofani, Ennio was able to affect enough confidence to get past the good Sister's suspicions. Evelina was thrilled to hear from him. The testament of her mother and father had provided for her to reside at St. B's while she attended classes and she did so because it was their wish. The flat they had owned would be waiting for her upon her graduation. Meanwhile, the young woman treasured her moments of freedom as much as any student in strict environs such as St. Benedict's would. She suggested to Ennio that they meet. She would bring her classmate Annabella because it would be that much more fun, and as a bonus, Sister would not question Evelina's going out alone. The three could glory in the passeggiata tradition, eat gelato, and forget their lessons for an hour or two.

The girls told Sister Leo that they were going to take a bus to Santa Maria in Trastevere for confession. The pair gathered their prayer books and rosaries and set out to meet Ennio in a charming square of shops outside the Vatican proper. Ennio was well acquainted with Annabella as she and Evelina had become instant friends on their first day at St Benedict's and she had been introduced to the priest in training shortly after.

There were warm hugs and air kisses all around when the three met on that temperate afternoon. They chattered happily throughout the bus ride to the Trastevere neighborhood. As soon as they departed the stubby, white vehicle, they purchased their sweets with money Ennio had collected by begging from his fellow seminarians. Coins were hoarded and hidden by schoolgirls and seminarians alike as neither in their respective rigidly monitored settings were allowed to hold much in the way of currency.

The carefree trio breathed deeply of the springtime air as they strolled without purpose along the streets near the church of Santa Maria, savoring the rare treat of their rich dessert before they went inside to take their turns in the confessional. Once they had rushed through their whispered prayers of penance, they dawdled for a while on the steps of the octagonal fountain outside the church. As the sun was setting, they stood and stretched before heading down a narrow, bricked alleyway of back entrances and trash cans. It was a shortcut to a café Ennio had heard about. Music, he'd been told, filtered from the cafe into the streets each night. It created a free concert of sorts for those without the means, or of an appropriate age, to enter the establishment. The three made their way along the narrow passageway in the increasing darkness, laughing and teasing in the playful way of the young on a happy outing. Evelina hesitated slightly when she noticed two figures approaching. She didn't feel particularly threatened even though there were no other people in the alley. It wasn't late, and Ennio was with them. When she felt Ennio also slow his stride however, she became uneasy. The group grew quiet. Ennio placed one arm around each girl, turned them, and steered them back the way they had come.

Evelina did not know how the two men could have moved so quickly. They were in front of her in an instant. In the dusk, their faces appeared distorted. As Evelina peered into the gloom, trying to make out features, one of the men grabbed her, dragging her away from her friends. She tried to scream but the man's grip around her body was so tight that she had no air with which to make a sound. She struggled with all her might but could not move. A black shape leaped toward her attacker and she realized it was Ennio just as the priest-to-be crashed into them. His effort released the man's grip long enough for Evelina to cough once and then scream out "Annabella!"

Ennio turned his attention to the other girl. The second man held Annabella's limp body in his arms like a child. As Ennio approached, he saw the hideous face of the girl's aggressor. The man's eyes were red and lifeless. Blood and bits of flesh hung from the sharp, pointed fangs that showed at the corners of his mouth. As Ennio ran toward the thing, it unceremoniously dropped Annabella's body on the ground. The wretch gave out with a long, sickening hissing sound before it ran around the corner and away. The other one, the vampyre, as Ennio now believed it to be, was squealing and limping away after his cohort.

Ennio, sensing it was too late to help Annabella, spun back around toward Evelina. To his surprise, a third man, wearing a knee-length black, fitted jacket, too warm for the weather, was holding Evelina upright. Ennio assumed from the man's garb that he was a priest and ran to the two. He stopped in his tracks when he saw the man's white face. It was one of the attackers' kind. Ennio shouted, "Put her down!"

"Quiet, you foolish boy," said the ghoul. It held Evelina

upright even as she clung to the thing. Ennio watched in horror. He called her name. He tugged at her. Evelina ignored her companion altogether and moved her arms up around the neck of the brute. When she looked into his burning green eyes and saw what Saverio was, she whimpered, "No."

Ennio pounded on Saverio who pushed the priest away with a smooth, easy motion. Ennio stumbled but did not fall. He watched, spellbound as Saverio's fangs retreated and his eyes changed into human-looking eyes. The phantom reached up and inch by inch pulled Evelina's arms from around its neck. It turned her, steering her into Ennio's waiting grasp.

"I am Saverio. I will take care of the assassins," said the vampire. And then he was gone.

CHAPTER 11
THE CHIROPTERA

The steadfast make their mindful way
With persistent pursuit of philosophy,
Hindered by apparitions
Of melting flesh and squealing bats.

The investigation into Annabella's death remained open for many months. Evelina and Ennio were crushed by grief and they anguished over their inability to do more than collect the poor girl's abandoned rosary and torn book of prayers on that awful night. It was never revealed in public that Annabella's body was found bloodless. In the end, her death was ruled an attempted robbery, resulting in a fatality. No one questioned why a thief would choose to prey upon a young woman still at her studies out for a stroll with friends. No mention was made in the papers, either, of the discovery of the two bodies found several blocks from Annabella's on the same night. They were men, lying in an unnaturally large river of blood, wooden stakes through their hearts, their heads ripped from their bodies. Ennio learned of the discovery through his Vatican sources. Many months later he shared his knowledge with Evelina in hopes, he told her, of impressing upon her the danger Saverio presented.

After this initial contact with diabolic beings she'd had no idea existed and the loss of her dear classmate, Evelina spent almost a month in hospital suffering from what her bewildered doctors described as a 'prolonged attitude of trauma'. Ennio was her constant visitor. He cared for her as he always had, offering comfort and guiding her to understanding and acceptance. The two talked for hours on end about their shared ordeal. Ennio read to Evelina from copies he had made of Vatican texts that he and just a handful of others were allowed to access. Evelina learned that Ennio had deduced at the start of the attack that the three were under siege by the soulless undead. She learned, too, of his terror at finding her in the arms of Saverio. As the months passed, Evelina would come to think of the aberrations that had taken the life of Annabella as she would any human murderer, dangerous and profane, but not fantastical.

When Evelina was able to leave the hospital, Ennio took her to visit Father Luca. In his ninety-four years, seventy-five of them ordained, Father Luca had seen much. He had fought every breed of spiritual and physical enemy imaginable on behalf of innocents like Evelina and poor Annabella. The elder of the church was a master at making the unbelievable sound commonplace. He wasn't a gloomy sort; he was ever optimistic that life and love would triumph over mortality and fear. And so he drew people in. He taught them that it was good to live and to laugh in defiance of the existence of unspeakable perversion. Through Father Luca's benevolence and humor, Evelina was able to believe, as she had before her rendezvous with the spiritual dark side, that grace did exist.

Evelina returned to school to finish her education a stronger, wiser young woman. She forever credited Father Luca and Ennio with helping her to recover her physical and mental health after the singular calamity of meeting evil face to face. She healed, but she did not forget. She did not forget Saverio. Even during the long intervals when his presence was not known or felt, she thought of him often. The one thing neither she, Ennio, nor even Father Luca could ascertain, was why a soulless, exanamite entity would rescue a young woman ripe with silky blood from others of his kind but not feed on her himself. Evelina often recalled the vampire's green eyes and the gentle way he lifted her to Ennio's arms. An unsettling sense of gratitude to Saverio tickled at her mind from time to time. But, whenever she started to think of his actions as benevolent, she would compel herself to recall the dismembered bodies of his brethren and horror would again engulf her. He was one of them, base and corrupt, never to be trusted. She must ever be on her guard because, and this was the most difficult thing to accept, he knew her.

In the years following their traumatizing introduction to the existence of the undead, Ennio and Evelina saw Saverio now and again. He hovered and watched them; they felt his presence. Once in a great while, he showed himself with eyes a̶l̶ ̶e̶ and fangs bared, but he never attacked or threatened When he did emerge from the gloom displaying this ᵥ aspect, he would glide; almost fly past them, leaving behind nothing but a hint of his distinctive, not unpleasant scent.

One early, misty evening in the late springtide that followed Saverio's dramatic entrance into their lives, Ennio walked Evelina to her dormitory. They had been to a local bookstore. Evelina had been buying gifts for her classmates in anticipation of parting for the upcoming term break. Ennio often accompanied Evelina on outings for safety's sake in those days, his various pockets filled with what his studies told him were protections against vampiric attack. An ornate metal flask filled with holy water that had been blessed by the Holy Father himself was in Ennio's vest and cloves of garlic filled his pants pockets whenever he went out. Evelina refused his attempts to transfer garlic to the pockets of her jackets. She always carried the old wooden rosary that her parents had given to her on her first communion day as her armor. She did not know how much protection it offered but it comforted her and she trusted in its spiritual energy. She considered her worn rosary the holiest of relics more for its connection to her mother and father than its having been blessed by a cranky old Bishop.

Ennio held his big black umbrella over both of them as they scurried along the narrow cobbled path that led to Evelina's dormitory building. As Ennio was about to grab the wrought iron rail of the stairs to the outer door of the yellowed stone structure, a flash of movement caught his eye from farther up the path.

Ennio stopped abruptly. He reached for Evelina's arm and pulled her into his side. Evelina followed his gaze to the figure ten meters or so ahead of them. It was Saverio. He stood with his body facing away from the two, his head rotated to an impossible degree. He was looking right at them. His russet hair was wet and in complete disarray. His eyes glowed brilliant green and his horrible fangs were bared, like those of a snarling wildcat. He raised one skeletal hand in the air and curled the long fingers with their long, dark, and pointed nails in a chilling gesture.

Ennio dragged a stunned, immobilized Evelina up the half dozen steps to the arched wooden door. It was not locked as it did not provide access to the building. It opened onto a small vestibule where the security system and heavier inner doors were kept locked to ensure the safety and sanctity of the women in residence. The seminarian pushed the outer doors open, standing to the side so Evelina could enter. He slipped in behind her and tossed his umbrella aside without closing it. Saverio, Ennio whispered to his companion, would not be able to enter the vestibule, having never been invited inside.

As the two discussed these events of the past in Evelina's cozy living room, Ennio admitted that he had never before that day at her dormitory door tested this bit of vampyre lore. He had guessed, he told his friend, that the dormitory itself would not be considered a public place because people lived in it. A translation of one ancient volume of Etruscan magic revealed that the undead could enter common areas without invitation. They believed this to be true based upon Ennio's anecdotal evidence. Over the months preceding he and Evelina's panicked retreat to the vestibule, Ennio had detected other vampyres and seen Saverio in several public places.

On that day in the dormitory entrance, Ennio prayed aloud that he had his information straight as he and Evelina looked out the windows of the double doors. The two saw Saverio move a few steps farther up the path toward the school, then reverse directions and float toward them. Evelina turned and frantically tried to work her key in the lock of the inner entryway. A fraction of a second later, Saverio's face appeared in one of the half-moon shaped windows of the anteroom doors. He faced Ennio, fangs showing, eyes burning. Ennio involuntarily jumped backward into Evelina. She spun around. Seeing Saverio's frightening visage not three feet away peering at her, she screamed and pressed herself against the locked door behind her. Ennio fumbled for the small bulbs of garlic in his pants pockets. For her part, Evelina was unable to look away from Saverio's features in the window. His palms were pushed onto the wet glass at either side of his face. He opened his mouth in a smirk made grotesque by the stretching of his lips over his long, pointed teeth. Evelina was mesmerized by the two drops of blood that grew longer and finally fell from one brilliant white fang until, in a single heartbeat, the entity vanished. He was not fleeing, not retreating, not even ambling away. He was simply not there.

Ennio reported to Evelina later that his walk back to the seminary grounds was free of any trace of Saverio. What he *had* seen was a sizable puddle of blood on the far side of the church that was situated just across the walkway from Evelina's dormitory building. The late-day sky was black with bats; as black as a moonless midnight. He was not able to explain to her what that meant. He did not know.

There were other times when Saverio presented himself to the two of them as a human man. There was nothing hideous or wrong about his face at these times. In fact, he was a man who would be considered rather beautiful, if he were not so dreadfully pale and thin.

Now and again, Evelina would look out her classroom window and see Saverio – the man – with his long coat flapping in the breeze. His hands would be casually in his pockets. He would be gazing toward the windows, smiling a small smile. At other times, Evelina judged the look on his face as he peered through the wavy glass of the tall school windows to be a pensive one. On days she saw Saverio on campus, Evelina would avoid the other girls when leaving class and venturing outside. The Saverio she saw from the safety of her classroom did not appear threatening. Even so, she never forgot what had happened to Annabella. If the vampire was on campus grounds for the purpose of making a young girl his victim, she wanted to ensure that she was that victim rather than another of her schoolmates. The safety of her fellow scholars was always of grave concern to her, but as her school years progressed, Evelina relaxed somewhat because no girls were attacked, nor did she ever hear rumors of her classmates being confronted by any type of odd or threatening being.

Ennio confided to Evelina that, on the other hand, he did have brushes with the dark entity. There had been instances when Saverio had swept past the priest-in-training on the streets of Vatican City, bumping the slight seminarian with his steely arm. Ennio would look up, startled to see the undead stalker's mocking smile.

On several occasions, the two had been out together and spied Saverio in the shadows. The vampire had ignored Ennio completely as he studied Evelina with extreme interest, like a cat ready to pounce. While Ennio never failed to maintain his outward calm at these times, Evelina suspected that these mutual encounters with the beast upset her friend more than any other.

In spite of their own continued meetings with Saverio, there never were any reports of attacks on the other girls in the school, nor were Ennio or Evelina molested by Saverio or any other of his kind. While they remained always on alert, the two lived their school days in a passably normal way.

When not occupied with classes, church, or school activities, they would spend an evening discussing whether or not they should turn the tables on Saverio and go on the hunt themselves. Should they attempt to do what Ennio had not yet done to any vampyre; put a wooden stake through Saverio's heart and end the terror of his stalking? Ennio insisted that he could not let Evelina be involved in such an action in any way. When she once suggested that she would make the ideal bait should it become necessary to draw Saverio into the open, Ennio shuddered. "No way, as they say, mia cara," he insisted. Saverio was the very denotation of elusive. Evelina was young and unpracticed; they both were. There was also the matter of Saverio's perverse magic to consider. Ennio reminded Evelina that she had been susceptible to Saverio's hypnotic wiles the night of Annabella's death.

There was another consideration as well. While there was ancient, and some not so ancient, documentation of Saverio's past deeds, the two of them had never witnessed him injuring a living human being. Should they wait until they had proof of his homicides, or was it safe to assume he slaughtered people and hunt him down like the monster he was reported to be? It felt to Evelina like an unsolvable quandary. Saverio had salvaged her life that night in the alley. She could not bring herself to wish for him to be murdered, no matter how much she feared what he might do. Even Ennio struggled with the idea as an ethical dilemma. He would readily stake the caitiff, he said, in the act of self-defense or to defend another. That being the case, tracking and killing a man, even one who was purported to be already dead, wasn't an idea he relished.

CHAPTER 12
THE MENACE

Lilting, luxurious tranquility Is fragmented by dangerous covetousness. Escalating acts of intimidation Dim the newborn light.

In time, Evelina graduated from the academy and threw herself into her work at the orphanage. Although Ennio had, by this time, taken his final vows, he continued his advanced studies. Within a matter of months, he was assigned to a parish where he could interact with parishioners and enjoy a somewhat routine everyday life. He did not know and did not ask if the fact that Evelina lived in an adjoining parish and within walking distance of his church, was a coincidence. The Vatican gave every exorcist a parish assignment. They feared that any healer, even one as steady as Ennio, could slip into depression or even insanity if he focused on the demonic to the exclusion of all else. Ennio's study of all things inhuman advanced even as he married couples, baptized babies and buried the righteous. He devoured every bit of information he could about the azoic organisms known through the ages as vampyres. The Vatican's exclusive library, he found, offered much to study even though the pertinent information was not easy to unearth amongst the one hundred fifty thousand historical volumes archived there. He found at least a dozen references to Saverio, some dating back hundreds of years. He related to Evelina that Saverio had been recorded to have been in a myriad of places, witnessed much history, and killed many, both human and supernatural.

Sightings of their tall, pallid stalker were less frequent than they had been during their school days until the publishing of Evelina and Gaetano's marriage banns. Since that milestone, Saverio had become increasingly bold about showing his face to Evelina and sometimes Ennio, his unsettling smile more mocking than ever. Evelina never saw him close to the orphanage. This may have been, she hypothesized, because she had reduced her working hours there for the duration of her engagement. With the increase of contact with the rogue, she worried about attracting evil to the children. Conversely, if she were walking in the park, or doing her shopping when the sun was low or under cover of clouds, Saverio would often materialize. Without warning, he would be beside her or in front of her. He might even speak.

"Working on our trousseau are we?" he taunted one gray, foggy day outside a dress shop where Evelina had stopped to look at a window display. His words were still an echo as he faded into the mist.

Just a week before the wedding, Evelina saw the voyeur approaching as she carried a well-filled canvas market tote in each hand toward the apartment she would soon share with Gaetano. It had gotten later than she cared to stay out alone, and the sun had dipped behind the buildings. Evelina hesitated, wondering what she could do. She knew that no evasive action would be effective. As she wavered, Saverio materialized in front of her. She was taking a step to the side as if to move around the vampire when he grabbed hold of her arms.

"The big day approaches," he said without his typical derisive smile. He searched her face. Evelina stood stock still and said not a word. "You are going to do this thing?" he prodded.

He wasn't hurting her. His manner was not aggressive. His face was human, his tone mild. She was fearful, but not panicked. The benign aspect of the creature notwithstanding, Evelina was uneasy enough, or intrigued enough to be rendered mum. She was gripped by Saverio's eyes even though they weren't glowing. Today they were just an unusual, riveting green. They were full of what looked like, but could not be human emotion. What emotion might that be, deliberated the captivated woman? *It is longing*, she decided. If he longed to end her and empty her body of its vital fluid, she wondered for the thousandth time, why he did not just do it? Why had he not done it at any time during all the years since their first meeting, indeed, why not *at* that first meeting? Evelina remained silent as she pondered these questions and Saverio eventually dropped his eyes to the ground. He slid his cold fingers deliberately down the length of Evelina's arms until they touched her hands. She gripped the handles of her bags more tightly though she trembled from his touch. A sound escaped him, something like the raspy, halting cough of a very elderly man. He removed his hands from hers and clasped them behind his back. This time the entity was not gone in the blink of an eye. Instead, Saverio stepped around the stunned Evelina and walked away. She stood still for several beats before turning to observe him placing one foot in front of the other, head lowered, ignoring the people around him. Evelina realized, *"he isn't on the hunt, he must have fed not long ago."* The idea made her shiver the rest of the way home, even though it was a balmy day.

CHAPTER 13
THE FRENZY

Entrails washed from the polluted cobblestones.
Be gone the gore, the soulless wail no more.
The resolution an unbridled obscenity;
A cruel rescue by a loathsome fiend.

Once the tales of preceding years and more recent days had been revisited, the particulars that Gaetano would need to hear were settled upon. With no more to say, Evelina and Ennio sat side by side on the rose leather sofa, holding hands like frightened children as they awaited Gaetano's arrival. He was late, much behind his time. The minutes felt endless to Evelina. Footsteps of other tenants came and went. With each noise from the hallway, she grew more restless. The clock ticked on and Ennio began to shift and sigh as well. Even his renowned patience was wearing thin.

Evelina was considering the idea that she and Ennio might

have to go on a quest to find her errant husband when the sound of Gaetano's key in the door came, causing the pair to jump from their shared seat. They dropped their joined hands. After a last look between them, Evelina breathed in deeply and said, "Sit Ennio. Things should seem as natural and ordinary to him as possible."

Ennio sat but pulled his torso up straight as Evelina approached the door. When Gaetano entered, she could tell right away that he had partaken of far too much wine. She supposed he had never returned to the office after the midday repast and had trifled away the rest of the workday in a drinking establishment. Her husband, meticulously groomed almost without fail, was disheveled. His strawberry-blond hair stuck out in all directions and he was badly in need of a shave. Worst of all, he gave off a sharp animal-like smell.

Evelina realized it was more than neglect of hygiene, and an afternoon in his cups that had Gaetano in such a disheveled and malodorous condition. His transformation had begun in anticipation of the coming full moon. *His confusion has led him to medicate himself with drink*, she speculated. This was understandable. Evelina hoped that it would not make she and Ennio's job that much more taxing. She was not sure it would be possible to convince even a sober Gaetano that his body was harboring a demon wolf.

"What are you doing here, Ennio?" Gaetano slurred.

"Evelina invited me to come by for a chat," replied Ennio in a calm, even voice.

Evelina, feeling there was no time and no reason to delay, took hold of Gaetano's arm. She led him to the flowered chair. He plopped into his seat and she smoothed the skirt of her dress as she sat back down beside Ennio. "Sit with us awhile, Darling. There are things Ennio and I must tell you."

"What the hell are you talking about Evelina? What is going on between you two? Are you conspiring against me? Are you in love with each other?" Gaetano rose, swaying from the drink.

Evelina was at the end of her rope after this tense day. She stood, too, and commanded, "Sit down, Gaetano. Don't be an ass. Be quiet and listen to us. Lives, including your own, may depend upon you hearing what we have to say."

This seemed to sober her wobbling husband somewhat. He removed his jacket, struggling with it only a bit in his lingering inebriation. He dropped back into his chair.

"So, what is the big secret you are keeping from me; this life and death mystery?" Gaetano's bravado was back for an encore.

"Gaetano," Evelina cautioned.

"Well, what? What is it?" Gaetano demanded as he looked from Evelina to Ennio, his eyes still a little unfocused.

Ennio warned, "What we have to tell you will be almost impossible to believe, Gaetano."

"Oh, for the sake of the good Lord, tell me already," Gaetano insisted.

"Yes, of course, of course." Ennio took a deep breath and went on. "Do you remember the scratch you received on your face at your wedding reception, Gaetano?"

"How do you know about that?" Gaetano challenged. His words still had a slight slur to them.

"No, Gaetano, just listen," interjected Evelina in the authoritative voice she had adopted for this mission.

Gaetano shot Evelina a look of surprise. He answered,

"Yes, Fabrice has not been right since she was just a young girl."

Fabrice, of course, Evelina was aggrieved by her inability to recall the lovely, haunted woman's name.

"In what way has she been not right, Gaetano?" Ennio pried.

Gaetano went on. "She was the victim of an attack by a vicious dog when she was still in school. Her injuries healed quite well but, I am sad to say, she never recovered in other ways. She has been only a shadow of her former self all these years, but she seems to have a unique fondness for me." He sighed, "It has always been assumed that it is because I was the one who found her and chased away the hound. Her behavior can be unpredictable, but I can't believe she would hurt anyone. It was just a scratch."

Ennio and Evelina glanced at each other with eyebrows raised before Ennio turned back to Evelina's perplexed husband.

"What kind of dog was it, Gaetano?"

Gaetano snorted. "I don't know. It was a huge animal; the biggest dog I've ever seen and no breed I knew."

"Go on, tell us more, Darling," urged Evelina.

"Well," her husband explained, "I heard screams from the garden of my zia's home. I ran to the sound and found Fabrice. The dog had pinned her to the ground. It was snarling and growling. Its fur was grey and so long that it flew about as it moved. When it became aware of me, it looked right at me. Its enormous eyes shone red in the moonlight. Before I could move, the thing ran off. It moved like lightning. It just leaped into the trees and was gone." I knew it was diseased; an animal with eyes like that."

"What you saw was not a dog, Gaetano. It was a wolf," said Ennio. "Not an ordinary wolf; a man that had become a wolf-like creature."

Gaetano stared at Ennio for several seconds before he burst into laughter. He still sounded somewhat tipsy. "Are you talking about werewolves, Ennio?" he confronted the priest. "You are either more drunk than I am, or you are insane. Your studies of the bogeyman have ruined your mind, mio amico."

"Werewolves and other monstrous beings do exist, Gaetano." Ennio was speaking in as calm and as steady a tone as he could muster. "Evelina and I have a story to tell you about how we came to know of them."

Gaetano gave a contemptuous grunt, but he listened as the two related the details of their first meeting with Saverio. The ambushed man's expressions changed from amazement to scorn and disbelief and then back again as the incredible tale unfolded. When the storytellers finished with the information that Saverio was often seen by them both to this day, Gaetano stared forward and was silent for a long moment. He shook his head in a wide arc from side to side. Finally, he declared, "You are both crazy."

Evelina tried to drive home the point. "Gaetano, you must believe your wife. I would not lie to you. Now you need to know about your own rendezvous with an entity others don't believe exists. Your cousin, Fabrice; we believe she is a werewolf, and you will become one at the next full moon because of that scratch."

At this Gaetano jumped to his feet. With one long stride, he was standing over Evelina. Ennio rose to intervene, but Gaetano catapulted him into the wall knocking the slight priest unconscious. Gaetano grabbed his wife by one arm. He jerked her to her feet and she screamed. Evelina's deranged husband let out a roar and covered her mouth with his large hand reaching the other around the back of her head. Releasing her cries for just an instant, he then clasped her about her throat with all ten fingers silencing her wails. Evelina struggled against Gaetano's steely grip. Her eyes, at first wide with horror at her husband's murderous countenance began to flutter as her vision grew dim. She could just make out that, behind Gaetano, Ennio was coming awake and trying to get to his feet. There was a noise in her head, a banging. Thump, thump, thump, thump, louder and louder it came.

Ennio was on his feet. He tottered toward the bookshelf and picked up a bust of Christ. Turning, he almost fell but then regained his footing. He swung the statue high and brought it down on Gaetano's head. The hollow plaster shattered. Gaetano was wholly undeterred. Shards of the statue flew at Evelina's face as the banging went on and on. She realized it was someone pounding on the sky-blue painted door when it broke from its hinges and fell into the foyer. In the hallway stood Saverio.

"Invite me, for God's sake. Invite me in," the visitant shouted. Evelina could not.

Ennio yelled, "Come in, Saverio!"

Saverio flew straight to Gaetano and brushed him away as if he was a doll full of cotton stuffing. The easy push broke Gaetano's grip but he hung onto Evelina's beloved rosary, pulling it from her neck. The seed-sized wooden beads rattled to the floor.

"You!" exclaimed Gaetano. He made a move toward Saverio.

The vampire knocked him to the floor with a blow no human man his size would have been able to deliver. Gaetano stayed. With one arm, Saverio caught Evelina as she was about to lose consciousness. With his other hand, he turned her head to one side. He brushed her silky, dark hair away with a careful stroke and then, all in one smooth motion, lowered his white face, eyes glowing, fangs bared, onto her throat. The last thing of which Evelina was aware was Ennio leaned against the wall, sinking to the floor with his face in his hands.

CHAPTER 14
THE ABERRATION

A black fog engulfs the furies.
Turbulent, tenebrous nightmares
Impede the coven's casting;
Pentagrams are rubbed out
And hexes are revoked.

Evelina was awakened by the soothing feel of a refreshing, cold cloth against her skin. She blinked twice and then her eyes flickered open to see Saverio's face above hers. There was no trace of the ghoul left about it. He looked like a man. He observed her with sympathetic, caring eyes. A slight smile on his lips revealed no sharp, pointed teeth.

"Am I dead?" said Evelina. Her words came out in a faint croak.

Saverio's smile broadened. He shook his head and said, "No, Evelina."

Her eyes opened wider. "Am I undead," she whispered?

A short laugh escaped Saverio at her question. *A vampyre laughing*, she mused. *What a wonder!*

He answered her, shaking his head again, "No, no, of course not. The only thing that has happened is that the poison of the wolf has been removed from your body through the wound your dear husband has left on your throat."

Evelina's brow furrowed. She queried in a feeble voice, "What do you mean, Saverio?"

"When a man is tainted by the claw of one who is wolf, he becomes another of its kind," Saverio explained. "A woman cannot be werewolf. When a woman is scratched or bitten by one corrupted such as your husband," he jerked his head toward Gaetano who was still slouched on the kitchen floor, "this woman will lose some of her mental faculties. She can never recover her former self." Evelina's eyes widened. "Do not fear. You, my darling, will remain perfectly sane. I removed the tainted blood. You are weak now but rest and do not worry. You will soon be well," finished Saverio.

Evelina looked around the room. She saw that Ennio was now on his feet and had begun cleaning up evidence of the melee. Keeping one wary eye on Saverio, the other on Gaetano, he glanced back and forth from one to the other as he picked up broken splinters of Jesus, tossing them into the wicker trash basket he carried. At the word "darling", he himself made a noise akin to a low growl even as he kept on with his busy work.

Evelina did, indeed, feel as weak as the proverbial kitten, and a newborn one at that. She didn't want to move from Saverio's arms. He held her across his lap the way her mother had when she was a little child. She felt safe though she knew it was folly. She told herself that she must remember what Saverio was as Ennio never tired of telling her. But, for now, she just wanted to rest and be held by him. He had delivered her from death, and worse; how could she not feel secure in his arms?

Her head ached. She felt it was less from the trauma to which she had been subjected than it was from wondering about this exact question. And so she dared to ask, "Why have you rescued me again and again, Saverio?" Ennio and even the stunned Gaetano froze to listen for the vampire's answer.

"One day, sweet Evelina, I will tell you all there is to know about me; about us," Saverio assured her. "There is something I need from you in return for my help," he went on. "In the fullness of time, you will learn just what it is. On that day, you will decide if it is something you can give to me. It must be your choice." Ennio moved with caution toward the two in the chair as their undead rescuer spoke.

"I want to thank you for saving my life again tonight," Evelina said quietly to Saverio.

Ennio heard. Fists clenched, feet planted he thundered, "No, Evelina! Saverio, you unholy miscreation, put her down. Why do you plague us?"

Saverio stood from the cozy chair, Evelina in his arms. He eased her onto the long sofa, making certain her head rested on the cushioned arm. He planted a gentle kiss on her forehead as Gaetano made sputtering, moaning noises from his place in the kitchen. Saverio stood and walked to the door. Evelina and Ennio watched his movements, he suspiciously, and she with a look of curiosity. Saverio turned at the threshold.

"As I said, tiny priest...in time." He tilted his mop of deep auburn hair toward the kitchen. "Tie up the husband," he reminded them. And, once more, he was gone.

CHAPTER 15
THE COVENANT

Banshees keen from within and without,
Exacting the reaper's revenge.
A pledge of demise, the promise of the grave
Extinguishes the torch of faith.

Following the stunned pause that typically resulted from one of Saverio's nebulous departures, Ennio did as he had been told. Gaetano offered almost no resistance as the rector tethered his arms and legs as tightly as he was able, using a length of rope pulled from the large black case he often carried. Like those of many of his profession, his satchel contained holy water and oil, a gospel, and a crucifix. It also held a number of effects that most of those called to the priesthood did not cart around with them. Few parish vicars needed a ready supply of wooden stakes or coils of rough rope.

Gaetano was still somewhat incapacitated by Saverio's

blow even an hour after it had been delivered. Though not combative while being fettered, he cried at frequent intervals and his anger returned in half-hearted spurts of weak growls and snarls. Evelina supposed he was now more perplexed than ever.

"Gaetano," Ennio snapped as he squatted in front of the bound man. Gaetano made eye contact with him, so Ennio rushed on. "Do you hear? Can you talk to me? We must agree to a plan for your safety and ours."

Evelina added in a small voice from the sofa where she was resting, now in a sitting position, "and for that of the innocents."

"Gaetano, do you understand me?" Ennio hollered, his face inches from Gaetano's.

"Yes, Ennio, I hear you; stop shouting. I believe you. I feel such strange things happening to me. I know I am a danger." Without meeting Evelina's eyes, he said, "I am so sorry my love." Looking up at his priest he whispered, "I could have killed her." Evelina heard the quiet words from her position on the sofa where she continued to feel Saverio's algid embrace, the sting of his sharp teeth, and a debilitating weakness from her ordeal.

"Could have? You nearly did, Gaetano," said Ennio in a practical tone. "And she is well aware of it. "Now you understand why we must restrain you until this phase of the moon has passed." Ennio helped Gaetano to his feet and held onto him as the hobbled man shuffled to the chair in the living room. The bustling curate then brought Evelina a glass of sweet, deep red wine, which she appreciatively drank. Afterward, he helped her to the bathroom and stood in the hall facing Gaetano. Evelina could sense her guardian right outside the door all the while she was inside. When she emerged, he hadn't moved. He helped her back to the sitting room where Gaetano was weeping in his chair.

"My poor husband, none of this is your fault. I don't hold you responsible for hurting me. You must be strong. We will find a way to break this curse and set you free from the influence of the wolf," Evelina comforted Gaetano as she knelt by the chair. "You must allow Ennio and I to decide what is to be done. Put your faith in us. We will do all we can to keep you safe from yourself and any destructive actions you might take." It wasn't quite her Sister Evelina voice, but she made herself sound confident and sure. This was for Gaetano's benefit since she had no idea if she and Ennio knew what they were doing. Father Luca was gone. He had died at almost one hundred years old without ever mentioning the curse of the wolf to them and Ennio surely hadn't had time to consult another exorcist since this morning. She was sure, too, that Ennio had never studied Gaetano's scourge the way he had vampiric and other demonic influences. Come what may, it was down to them; one untried exorcist, and a much-weakened empath, to protect Gaetano and his potential victims. Knowing this, Evelina decided that she may as well behave as if she knew what she was about.

"I will listen, Evelina." Gaetano had become meek and obedient. He may have been willing to do as the two advised, but his words were followed by a low growling sound that made Evelina back a little bit away from him. "What are we to do?" he bid them as he regained control of his human voice.

Ennio spoke up. "There is a room in the sub-basement of the church. It would seem to have been a burial chamber." He hurried to add, "There are no longer any coffins or remains there." When Evelina let out her breath in a sigh of relief he went on. "The area has an iron grate for a door. It locks securely and is solid enough that I find it quite difficult to open and close. I have collected heavy chains to further secure the gateway. We will take you there tonight and lock you in, my friend. You will abide there until the full moon has passed and you have returned to your natural state."

Gaetano nodded in agreement. Tears rolled down Evelina's cheeks as she listened to Ennio's plan but she knew that it was the only way. They had a responsibility, born of their knowledge of Gaetano's circumstance, to make certain he assaulted no one else and created no more beasts cursed by the wolf. Gaetano cleared his throat and then said, in almost his normal voice, "Evelina, I would like to speak with Ennio alone."

"Of course, Darling," Evelina agreed. She rose and walked, unassisted this time, down the hallway toward the bedroom. She stopped as soon as she knew the two men could no longer see her.

She held her breath until Ennio began, "I know what you want to say, Gaetano."

"Let me say it, then," replied Gaetano in a low throaty voice, his ire resurfacing. When he spoke again, the anger seemed to have ebbed. Evelina peeked around the wall of the hallway to see him look directly into Ennio's worried, sapphire eyes. "Promise me, mio amico. Should I escape, you must do away with me. You must not let me injure my beloved. Please do not let me hurt anyone at all."

"Believe me, Gaetano, that has always been my plan. You will not mistreat our Evelina. You will not hurt another.

While I have not studied the werewolf for long, I know there are ways to kill you, if kill you I must. I am preparing," Ennio assured him.

"Thank you," Gaetano said with a faint exhale. Evelina thought he sounded relieved. That such a promise eased his mind broke her troubled, aching heart.

"I must know something," Ennio quizzed the still captive Gaetano. "You recognized Saverio when he burst in here tonight upon my invitation, did you not? When and where have you crossed paths with him?"

"In Paris," replied Gaetano. "It was on the last evening of our honeymoon. Evelina fainted in the street from hunger and heat, and that thing picked her up and brought her to me. He placed her in my arms, then walked away without explanation." Gaetano seemed to be considering something. He murmured almost to himself, "I remember wondering that day how a slight man such as he could carry even my petite Evelina." He snorted. "I don't know how he could have knocked me into the kitchen in that way."

Evelina walked back into the room and listened as Ennio explained. "A vampyre, newborn to the spiritless life, has the strength of two men. The longer it lives and feeds upon blood, the stronger it becomes. The earliest reference to the vampire Saverio that I have found is from a parchment believed to have been created in the second half of the fifteenth century. By now, his strength is no longer measurable."

"Yet he can be so gentle," Evelina said with a wistful sigh, making her return known to the two men.

Both turned to gape at her. Gaetano's mouth hung open in consternation while Ennio looked as if he had stepped in something unpleasant. "A gentle vampyre," the cleric protested, "I hardly think so."

Ennio stood. "We must delay no longer," he pronounced. "Evelina, are you strong enough to accompany us to the church? I don't want to leave you here now that Saverio has the ability to enter. You don't even have a door to lock against ordinary intruders."

"I can make it," she assured him. She changed from her wrinkled, bloodstained sundress into casual, faded-blue slacks and an oversized white shirt. She sat back down stifling a groan, put on her sneakers, and told the men she was ready. She *was* prepared to proceed. Not only that, but she was determined to prevent Ennio from keeping his morbid promise by seeing her precious Gaetano safely through his crucible.

"I pray we are *all* ready," Ennio's grim expression belied his hopeful petition. "Gaetano, I will have to untie your legs so you can walk. Will you come along with us? Will you cooperate?"

"Yes," Gaetano said. "But we must go straight away. I can feel my mind and body shifting. It is so strange. Muscle feels like it is detached from the bone and is moving about." He sounded bewildered and frightened. "I'm not angry but I feel like a man gone mad; wild! I don't want to flee or attack. I just don't know how much longer I will be able to control this thing within me." Gaetano, even with the hour of his transition growing closer, seemed to be gaining a better grasp of his situation. Evelina was grateful that he was able to reason in his current state. If he could not, she brooded, there would be no hope for their plan or her husband.

And so, final preparations were made. Evelina called the

building superintendent and gave a ridiculous excuse for the shattered door frame. She surprised herself by lying so expertly and easily. Desperate times call for desperate measures she told herself and her God. Gaetano's legs were untied and the three exited the building through a secure back door that was meant for resident use only. They agreed it would be wise to avoid the young man who sat at the security desk in the lobby.

Their heartrending odyssey to the church was uneventful, excepting Gaetano's periodic growls at wandering pets. Evelina cringed at the hideous, bass snarls that came from somewhere deep inside her good-natured husband. Thankfully, they passed by no human mortals to notice their odd procession. Nor did any black shadow follow them that Evelina could discern. She concluded that Saverio must have decided to trust them to cope with Gaetano. Either that or the vampire had important business elsewhere. Had his taste of her blood been sufficient nourishment or was he still hungry after his busy afternoon? Evelina shuddered at the idea. She looked up at the bewitching and terrible, waxing moon. She had once regarded the awful orb as something romantic. Later, she grew to appreciate its illumination when she feared Saverio might come for her at any time. Now, the glowing oval seemed a sinister entity. It represented heartbreaking, horrible death; the death of her happiness, the death of the guiltless and, should she fail, the death of her husband when it finally shone full and round on the midnight indigo of the Tiber.

CHAPTER 16
THE SEPULCHER

Ever downward they creep,
Step by creaking step,
Surrounded by decomposing loam.
The earth awaits a putrid quietus
And is filled with gruesome certainty.

The hour had grown late. No other corporeal soul was nearby to notice the married couple and their pastor enter the church. Once in the narthex, the three turned to the right instead of passing through the tall wooden doors of the chapel. In the far corner was a staircase leading to the lower level of the church. The huddled group started down. The wooden steps creaked but were covered in a worn, mottled blue carpet. There were no echoing footsteps to be heard even if there had been anyone else in the building. Gaetano tripped once but Ennio kept him from falling and they reached the bottom without injury or further incident. Aided by Ennio's boxy, red electric torch, they crossed the area of the basement now used primarily for storage. The brick walls were lined with statues of saints and ugly representations of the Christ looking devastated as he pointed to his broken, sacred heart. In the harsh glow of the lamp's beam, these works of art appeared garish and grotesque. In Evelina's mind, the saints' expressions offered no comfort or kindness; they accused her. She felt judgment and nothing else. She detected no hint that any of the glorified souls depicted in the sculptures, or who had died in the defense thereof, were prepared to help the three in their time of dire need. "*We are in every sense alone now; abandoned by God,*" she concluded. In the next instant, Evelina regretted having even considered such an idea. She said a quick act of contrition in her heart for her faithlessness.

The clustered trio passed through the kitchen area where countless funeral dinners had been prepared. Gaetano was forced to duck as they proceeded through the kitchen proper into a low-ceilinged pantry filled with canned goods and food preparation supplies. On the farthest wall of the small room was a marred relic of a dark-stained wooden door. A white metal cabinet with rounded edges and chrome handles was sitting about three feet in front of the forbidding entrance. There was a rusty pattern of the cabinet on the tile where it must have sat for a very long time. Evelina realized that Ennio had been in the pantry earlier and moved the cabinet out to reveal the imposing entryway to the ante-room he had found. Ennio lifted the primitive, wooden latch of the thick door and pulled it open with both hands and no small amount of effort. He searched the dark with his lamp for the crude stone steps that descended to the crypt where Gaetano must spend the next few days.

A stale and musty odor assaulted Evelina's nostrils as soon as the aged door swung open. A wave of nausea overtook her. She backed up until she was in front of the huge porcelain sink that was the centerpiece of the kitchen. Hanging on to the sweating surface of the sink's edge with both hands, she leaned low over it and retched bile until her legs were shaking. Ennio held his big beam torch in one hand offering the only illumination of the area. With the other holding fast onto Gaetano's tied wrists, he stood helplessly by as his helpmate coughed and splashed her face with metallic smelling water. "Evelina?" he urged, as Gaetano emitted a long, low whine.

The unsteady woman nodded and then wobbled her way back into the pantry. She followed as Ennio guided Gaetano down the narrow set of steps. She had the awful notion that the hunched and bound Gaetano looked like a judged man being led away for crimes already committed.

The cell Evelina's tall husband was expected to occupy for the night was no more than three meters square. It was just big enough for a coffin bier and a few mourners. The walls were of yellowed stone and the floors hard-packed dirt. There were niches carved into the walls for the storage and display of the deceased's posthumous wealth. This must be the reason for the locked grate, Evelina surmised. The words "grave robbers" bounced around in her mind making her feel even more anguished and ill.

It was apparent that Ennio had not squandered the middle hours of this long day in contemplation as she had. The dark, dank, and horrible room was fitted with a thin, narrow mattress covered in blue ticking, a gray woolen blanket, and a chamber pot. Evelina supposed the earthen pot would not be needed once Gaetano's change was complete. Her beautiful, dear husband would soon be a wild thing, with no need for human conveniences.

In the small area outside the crypt sat one wooden chair next to a white painted table with a round top not much larger than a dinner tray. Cluttering the dilapidated bit of furniture, Evelina counted four flashlights of various sizes. Next to them sat a stack of books bound in worn leather covers.

Ennio spoke. "We will stay here with you, Gaetano, and attend to your needs. We will guard you when," he trailed off before finishing with, "it happens. Evelina, you must tell me when you need air or anything else. Do not try to be stoic. You are not well. But," he paused in uncertainty, "do you feel you can handle things without me for just a short while? I do have some more arrangements to complete."

Gaetano was scratching at the floor with his banker's shoes and sniffing. His nose pointed toward first one and then another corner of the room. Evelina looked at her husband rather than at Ennio. One of the tears that had been threatening since they left the apartment escaped her eye. "Yes, we will be fine here for a bit. What must you do?"

Her old friend would not look at her. She persisted, "Do not keep secrets from me, Ennio."

The efficient cleric untied the cords binding Gaetano's hands, dropped them to the floor, and led him into the crypt, still saying nothing. The bedeviled man crawled onto the mattress and kicked off his expensive shoes. He curled himself into a ball and panted. Through his ragged breathing, he was able to get out the words, "So...sorry...Lina."

"Darling, you needn't be sorry for anything," Evelina insisted. "This is not your fault in any way. You are more a victim than any of us in this. Do not be frightened. Ennio and I are here for you. We will help you in any way we can. We won't let you come to harm." Evelina was doing her best to reassure her poor husband. She meant every word she said, even though her sick heart told her that she had no idea if she would be able to keep her promises.

Ennio anchored himself into the floor and pushed with his shoulder against the crypt doors, wrestling them closed. Evelina came up close to Ennio's ear as he worked his heavy chains through the bars of the cell. "Tell me where you are going and what you are planning, Ennio. Can you not see that I *must* know? How can I discern what is to be done if you evade me?"

Ennio took a breath and held it a moment. "Yes, you should know," he agreed with an exaggerated exhale. He hesitated a few beats and then explained, "The church has long agreed with the belief of the ancients that the element of silver holds metaphysical powers. This morning, after you left, I did obtain a gun. I did not bring it to your flat," he quickly interjected as a dark cloud of dismay spread over Evelina's face. "I did, however, take it to a gunsmith. He forged for it two silver bullets."

Evelina was crying without pretense now. She turned her head to watch Gaetano as he twitched and growled on his thin mattress. She stepped forward, clasped two bars of the ugly cell, and rested her head on them. Ennio went on. "I did not want the gun in this room until Gaetano was secured behind these bars. I didn't know how willing he would be to enter the cell. I could not predict his level of desperation. I would never have used the horrible thing on him in his human form. My fear was that he would try to use it himself. Please believe me, Evelina."

The jailing of the man in metamorphoses concluded with the loud clang of a giant padlock snapping into place. The cleric tested the lock once and then stepped toward Evelina. He lifted his hand to her chin, turning her head to face him, "You can surely see that I am trying my best to keep Gaetano safe. But, mia darling one, I have promised your husband I will do what must be done. I have no choice. I must keep that promise," he insisted. "We cannot let him leave this room until he is man again. If these bars and chains will not hold him, I need to stop him in any way I can."

"You will not kill my husband, Ennio," Evelina sobbed as she turned her whole body toward Ennio and grabbed his upper arms. "He is a man, not a demon," she cried. Then, lowering her voice to an angry hiss she went on. "He is not an evil thing. Even if he becomes a vicious wolf, he will be a man again and you cannot murder him!"

"I'm so sorry, my darling." Again, Ennio hesitated and then stated almost matter-of-factly, "The greater good."

Gaetano stirred then from his curled position and Evelina turned back toward the bars of his hideous cage. He yelped out, "What must...be done. And then, louder, "YOU." Evelina jumped at Gaetano's raised voice. He shook his head several times until he regained a bit of control and continued in a lower voice, "love...ever." The young couple's eyes met for a moment. And then her young and charismatic husband howled in a way that made Evelina feel as if her bones were coming apart and rattling around in her body. She covered her ears and closed her eyes until the sound no longer reverberated through the chamber.

As the hideous space returned to the relative quiet of Gaetano's panting, Ennio spoke. "Please look at me, Evelina," he pleaded. After a long moment, she did. His intense blue eyes searched her face for sympathy with his plight. He made his case. "As nearly as I can tell, there is no cure for Gaetano's affliction. Further, if he is loose, he *will* hunt. It is inevitable. I have raw meat for him and perhaps that will satisfy him enough that he will not try to escape. If he does get out, I will do what I can to subdue him. But, darling Evelina, what if he kills me? What if he injures me, and I too become the wolf? What then mi amore?"

He continued without mercy even as Evelina doubled over with grief and sobbing. "A werewolf can be killed by a silver bullet through the heart or by the total obliteration of its heart or its brain. Nothing else can stop it. Evelina, what would you have me do?"

"Mother of Mercy, help me," Evelina moaned. "Go, Ennio, go. Get your gun and your magic bullets. I hate you, Ennio, I hate you," she finished with a whisper.

"Darling, I know that you do. It is good that you do. I understand." Ennio lifted Evelina upright and wrapped his arms around her tired shoulders rocking her to and fro. He shushed and cooed as he helped her to sit on the spindly, cushion-less chair. He smiled a sorrowful smile and handed her his handkerchief. "I will return in a short while," he said.

As he turned to the uneven steps, Evelina reached out and grabbed the dull black sleeve of his shirt. "Ennio?" she entreated.

"Mia Evelina," he replied. "I know, I do know. Try to

breathe and rest a bit." She listened to his hollow footsteps retreat. Dropping her head onto her folded arms where they rested on the edge of the inadequate table, she closed her eyes and tried to take a deep breath. The moldy stench of her surroundings made such a thing next to impossible. Instead, she matched her inhales and exhales to the rhythm of Gaetano's ragged panting and whimpering. Her efforts did nothing at all to ward off the anguish of the endless day.

CHAPTER 17
THE SAVAGERY

In stainless preparedness for grisly homicide,
An amulet of piercing pain
Resplendent in offensive glory,
Lies, tawdry in its polished beauty.

Ennio returned after a short while with a carafe of water, blankets, the horrible, raw, ground meat, and, of course, the gun. It was a grotesque, chrome looking thing, and bigger than Evelina would have presumed necessary. She wondered if Ennio had any idea how to use such an instrument. *Perhaps marksmanship has been part of his training*, she pondered. *Maybe it is something deemed necessary for his life of facing evil in its primordial forms.* Before this night, Evelina would have guessed that crosses and holy water were the only weapons Ennio knew how to use.

"Is it loaded?" She challenged him.

"Yes, a bullet made from pure silver is in the chamber." He

reached into the pocket of his black vicar's pants, "here is the second." He placed the thing on the table beside the other accoutrements.

Evelina looked away. "Cara," said Ennio, "I want you to go upstairs to my rooms and rest. It will not be until tomorrow when the moon rises that Gaetano's transformation will be complete. Let me watch and wait. I have a pill that will help you sleep."

Evelina opened her mouth to argue. She looked at her husband asleep on his sorry narrow mattress. Drool ran from the corners of his mouth while his long legs twitched. Guttural sounds erupted from his throat at intervals. Too tired to protest, she decided to do as Ennio proposed but she wasn't ready to run along as told, no questions asked. "Where did you get the pill, Ennio?" she pushed him.

"It was given to me by a parishioner," replied the priest. He did not try to hedge. He looked into her eyes. "She is a physician with the coroner's office. She is quite skilled and eminently discreet."

"My, you do think of everything," replied Evelina with an odd half-smile. She walked to Gaetano's cage. She whispered it to avoid waking him. "I love you, my dearest." After a breath or two, she turned away and, without a glance in the direction of her old friend or another word, started up the stairs.

CHAPTER 18
THE ACROPOLIS

The strangling incense of October roses
Within the mausoleum walls
Overpowers the freshness of the shroud
And the eyes of the corpse still stare.

E velina had been given the grand tour of the rectory when Ennio moved in two years ago and knew where to locate his rooms. She found a small plate of saltines and a green ceramic bowl full of strawberries on the nightstand in Ennio's stark bedroom. Beside these sat the round, white pill, and a sweating glass of water. She was grateful for the pill and swallowed it with a sip of the cool water. She could do no more for her amato marito in her current state of exhaustion. While she had hoped to be able to rest without the artificial aid, she ached all over and craved the release of sleep. She assumed the pill would help; she prayed that it would. She removed her slacks and shirt, tossing them across the foot of the bed.

A white ceramic bowl and pitcher sat on a washstand in the corner. Beside them had been placed a threadbare but clean and neatly folded towel that was decorated with a faded print of pink roses. Evelina used these accessories to wash up as the little priest had obviously intended. Afterward, she pulled back the plain, white coverlet and crawled into Ennio's sheets. They smelled freshly laundered. What a busy man he was. She thought of him, his energy and his devotion. She knew he loved her and that he wanted to help her, care for her, and keep her safe. He was trying so hard. Yet tonight she could not be grateful to him. Her head told her that he was doing exactly what he was duty-bound to do and nothing more than what he had promised Gaetano. Her heart, on the contrary, told her that her oldest defender was plotting the destruction of the man she had promised to love always. That heart was filled with anger and grief. Was she to ignore the fact that Ennio had made his promise to Gaetano well after the horrible plan had been formulated and the mechanics of it set in motion? Evelina's head spun with disturbing, violent images. She tried to pray as she tossed and turned on the small, rigid mattress. At intervals, she wept, her tears staining Ennio's pillow.

Her rosary beads had been lost in the fracas at her home. Even the crucifix had been pulverized by Gaetano's sizable shoe and so she counted one Hail Mary on each finger. Sometime during the fourth sorrowful mystery of her whispered rosary, the medication took effect and she drifted off. She dreamed of blood and monsters; nonetheless, she slept.

CHAPTER 19
THE GAUNTLET

The lost, the missing, the almost and undead,
While unwitting history persists,
As winged spirits to the flame
Take treacherous flight
And evanesce to wisps of smoke.

A s Evelina awoke, the sun shone in through the blue and white checked curtains covering the single window of Ennio's spartan room. She eased herself up into a sitting position and stretched. Her body ached, and her head swam from the ordeal of the previous day. She took a few deep breaths in an attempt to get her system moving. She sat listening to faraway noises of banging pots for a minute or two and then stood to pull on her slacks. After dressing, she used the facilities across the hall from Ennio's room. She splashed her face again and again with cold water from the washbasin as if trying to wash away all the anxiety and confusion of the previous day. She smoothed her hair in the cracked mirror above the tiny pedestal sink. When she was as ready as she felt she ever could be, Evelina made her way to the rectory kitchen.

The housekeeper, Tia, said nothing except "Good morning, Miss," as Evelina pulled a glass from the cupboard. As she helped herself to some milk from the refrigerator and drank it sitting on a chair covered in red vinyl at a red-topped metal table, Evelina wondered if a woman emerging from the second floor of the rectory at this time of the morning was a common occurrence. This was Rome; full of clergy of all ages, nationalities, and sets of priestly standards. Tia was in her sixties now. She had likely seen it all, supposed Evelina, with the probable exception of what was going on beneath her church right now.

Evelina waited for Tia to leave the room before slipping out the door. Bone-weary, she limped down the short walkway to the church and let herself in the side door through which the servers entered the sacristy to prepare for Mass. She turned to the basement stairway thinking of the day she had hidden in that narrow room behind the altar just a few short weeks ago. She had entered from the social hall on the other side of the church and secluded herself there after another confrontation with Saverio. He had been the only danger Evelina had feared on that day. She could not have known that there was a much greater one at hand in the form of a sad little woman, a victim herself, utterly unaware of the pernicious disease she carried.

Evelina wondered where the vampire who had first warned her that this day was coming, the one who had, just the previous day safeguarded her life once again, might be at this moment. What was he doing on the day that would bring the full moon as she made her way through the empty kitchen to the pantry and the steep, dark stairs that led to Gaetano's dungeon? Did Saverio care if Gaetano died? Would he feel anything if her husband took her life or Ennio's? Would he care about the deaths of whatever number of innocent people a werewolf might eviscerate of a moonlit night? She supposed not, since he, too, poached the innocent for sustenance. He seemed yesterday, once again, to have empathy for her, at least. If he did care, had his confidence in the abilities of Ennio increased since he had last taunted the curate about his ineffectuality? *Saverio was nothing if not mysterious*, she thought, as she let out a dispirited sigh and shoved open the door that led to the underground tomb.

As Evelina cautiously descended the deteriorating steps, frightful snarling sounds emanated from the vault and grew louder as she approached. She found Ennio asleep with his head wedged in next to the volumes on the rickety table. Around him echoed a cacophony of brutal, tortured sounds made by a creature she knew must be Gaetano rattling the bars and chains of his prison. As she stared wide-eyed at the thing that was her husband, she watched hairs sprout on his face and his upper body. The coarse fur grew longer by the second. The straw-colored mane on his head was three times longer than it had been the night before and in the murky atmosphere of the sub-basement, it exhibited a sickening green cast. His shirt was a torn rag lying on the floor. The chamber smelled as if it were inhabited by a pack of filthy, wet dogs and Evelina suppressed a gag.

She went to Ennio and shook him awake. "What is happening? Is this it?" she barked.

"No. According to all I have read, Gaetano will not be every inch a wolf until the moon rises. That will not happen until well after the sun sets. This is just the beginning," came Ennio's groggy reply.

Evelina did not suggest Ennio leave his post to sleep. She was not prepared to give him any sympathy. "Fine, we will wait," she said. And they did. All through the long day, they sat, or they paced. They tried to tempt Gaetano with the meat, its rank smell choking Evelina. They placed a tin cup of water inside the bars of his prison. He took no notice of their offerings. Whenever they approached he retreated to the corners of his enclosure and growled at them. His snarls showed too many, too sharp teeth.

The pair of sentinels took turns going up to the kitchen or outside for short-lived intervals of rest. They heard the muffled arrivals and departures of the faithful attending the Mass celebrated by Ennio's associate, Father Gerard. They wondered aloud if the Mass-goers heard Gaetano's intermittent howls or the banging of the bars of his enclosure as he threw himself about in the cramped space. At any rate, no one came looking for the source of the racket. At least no one found it.

Evelina went up to the rectory church office, once, to call Gaetano's employer. She told the kind woman the truth that Gaetano was ill. He would not be at work for the rest of the week, Evelina added. She prayed zealously that her husband would survive this awful night and still be in need of employment. Even as she made Gaetano's excuses, she feared the possibility that he would never again walk through the door of the bank, cappuccino in hand, smiling and greeting his co-workers. This bitter reflection broke her heart anew.

CHAPTER 20
THE TRANSMUTATION

Broken bones and mangled flesh,
Shattered skulls and splintered spines,
Vicious execution without prejudice;
Ubiquitous atrocity.

As the day wore short, Ennio checked the pocket watch he had inherited from Father Luca at shorter and shorter intervals.

"Stop that, Ennio, you are making it worse," snapped Evelina. "What difference does the hour make? It will happen when it happens."

Ennio did not answer but put the watch back into his pocket. They waited. The church above them was quiet. Unfortunately, their hideaway was not. Gaetano howled and snarled. He screamed and rattled his prison door. Sometimes he sounded like a man in abject agony. Sometimes he sounded like a provoked vicious animal.

Several more times, Evelina approached the cage thinking she would offer her husband comfort. She was disheartened when her movements proved only to further agitate her poor Gaetano and she ultimately stopped trying.

After what felt to Evelina like a century of listening to the horrible sounds and inhaling the nauseating stench of the room, Ennio suggested she go up to the kitchen window to watch for the moon. Evelina knew that Ennio was aware of the exact minute of the moon's rising and that his ruse was an attempt to give her a brief reprieve. She went along with the notion that her visual confirmation would be helpful in some way, and, with weary steps, started up to the kitchen.

At the top of the steps, she pushed open the heavy door to the crypt and with a shove of her posterior closed it behind her. She stepped around the metal cabinet and into the open room. The air around her smelled of old cooking and musty basement. Still, it was refreshing to her after the strangling miasma of the crypt, and she took a long, deep breath. Emerging from the pantry, she could see that the high windows of the church kitchen were dark. She went to the nearest of the windows, picking up an aluminum folding chair of the type found in church halls around the world, from a neat stack along the wall. Opening it, she placed the chair below the narrow window pushing down on the smooth metal several times to make sure her makeshift step was stable. She climbed up for a better look at the eastern sky. Detecting a glow between the buildings on the skyline, she stood enthralled, watching; waiting. One minute passed, then another. Before the third had ticked away the first crescent of the yellow sphere broke the surface of the slice of the horizon that she could see. When it did, she heard Gaetano emit a high pitched, piercing wail. It set her teeth on edge and sent tremors up and down her spine.

Evelina jumped from her unsteady perch and hurried back to the big door with the awful secret behind it. Dragging the behemoth open once more, she paused at the top of the stairs. Gaetano's growls, though interspersed with whimpers and human-sounding coughs, were growing louder.

And then, all at once, Evelina was engulfed in silence. The calm, after the long day and night of her husband's storm of angry, tormented eruptions was more unnerving to Evelina than the noise. At a snail's pace, she descended the stairway, her shaking hands sliding down the walls to keep her upright. When she reached the bottom, she froze, staring at her husband. From her place against the wall of the chamber, well away from the cage door and his lethal claws, she could see that Gaetano's face was changing shape. Evelina mistrusted the evidence of her eyes. *How can this be?* The reality of Gaetano's conversion was unfathomable.

Her husband no longer had the countenance of a man. What could only be called a snout grew from his face as Evelina watched, paralyzed with terror. From her vantage point, she could hear the squelching and rasping of flesh tearing and reforming as Gaetano's eyes opened wider and wider. The whites almost disappeared. The small bit of space that showed around his golden irises was blood red. His teeth were lengthening in the way Evelina had seen Saverio's retreat. But these were not the pointed tools of the vampyre. These teeth were thick and curved like those of a gigantic dog; teeth meant to tear flesh and crush bone.

Evelina sensed Ennio standing from his chair at the minuscule table, "This is it, Evelina," he proclaimed.

"Yes, Ennio, I can see that," she replied, with an edge of sarcasm evident in her strangled voice. She glanced toward Ennio and saw him pick up the gun from the table. Through clenched teeth, she hissed, "Don't do it, Ennio, don't you do it."

Just then, Gaetano shook his whole body as a dog does as it leaves the water. He opened his mouth wide and let out a horrific, unearthly scream. Evelina saw a terrifying array of wolf's teeth impossible for a man to hold in his mouth. The thing that had been Gaetano threw his body at the bars that contained him, and the bars bent. Ennio yelled, "Run, Evelina! Go now!"

"I won't. I won't leave him," she shouted back, as she stood her ground.

The massive lycanthrope charged the bars once more and they gave way. Gaetano sprang toward Evelina. Enormous teeth came flying toward her. Eyes full of lustful violence revealed the intent of the animal. Even as she faced the mortal danger of her rabid husband unleashed, Evelina was aware of Ennio fumbling with the pistol. "No, Ennio!" she screamed. A shot cracked through the air. The Gaetano wolf staggered away from her. A red stain was spreading through the long hair just below the giant beast's neck. Evelina judged that the bullet had entered too high to have hit Gaetano's heart. The wolf-man teetered but kept his footing. Evelina ran to Ennio and grabbed his arm, trying to keep him from reloading the gun. Ennio shook her off with grim determination. Gaetano crouched on his haunches preparing to lunge again. Through the ringing of her ears, Evelina heard the chamber of the gun click into place. She took one step toward the wolf with the idea of shielding it from Ennio's silver bullet. But as she moved toward it, the animal that had moments ago been her beloved husband leaped at Evelina. Another shot exploded in the claustrophobic chamber. Gaetano let out a piercing howl. Evelina covered her ears and slumped to the ground as the wail rose and then fell. The cry with which Gaetano's body hit the packed dirt floor of the room was that of a human man. Bright red blood poured forth from the chest of what was, once again, suddenly, inexplicably, Evelina's young and handsome husband. The shiny projectile had hit its mark.

Gaetano now looked at his wife with the same loving eyes she had seen at the altar on their wedding day. He opened his mouth. He tried to speak, but nothing more than a faint gurgling sound came out as blood trickled from the corner of the soft human lips Evelina had kissed a thousand times with affection and with boundless ardor.

Evelina rose to her hands and knees and crawled to her beloved. She picked up his head and cradled it in her lap. "Gaetano, my Gaetano," she sobbed, her tears falling on his face.

Her husband's lips moved in silent effort. Evelina held her ear close to his mouth, her hair falling across his forehead. She thought she heard the words, "bless you." Gaetano died then, in Evelina's arms.

Evelina sat as if rooted to the spot for a full minute, listening. As the truth of the circumstance settled upon her, she began to sob and rock the body of her husband. The gun thudded against the floor as Ennio threw it away from him. Through her low keening, she could hear Ennio breathing hard and crying harder. For once, another person's anguish did not touch Evelina's heart. She could not care about Ennio's misery.

Long minutes later Evelina grew still. She was drained of tears, her body dehydrated and weak. The pulsing adrenaline from the terrible climax of Gaetano's transformation and its tragic end had dissipated, leaving her, once again, limp with fatigue. In an almost trance-like state of shock, she lowered Gaetano's head to the rock-hard, cold floor of the sickening chamber with an abundance of care. Placing one foot on the unyielding earth she pushed herself to a standing position and turned to Ennio who was sitting on the floor weeping into his hands. She leaned over him. Her voice growing louder with each word, she cried, "I loathe you, you murdering devil." She had never said such a hateful thing to another person, yet her voice rose further, and she ranted on. "You knew you would kill him, Ennio, you knew. You knew, did you not?"

Ennio struggled to stand. When the two were face to face he whispered vehemently, "No, no, no Evelina, I did not." He wavered as Evelina stared him down, her jaw tight with anger and strain, "But a werewolf rarely lives a long life," he rambled on, his eyes pleading for her sympathy. "As you saw for yourself, they have a ponderous, preternatural strength. They are wild in every respect in their transformed state. As we've also seen, they are extremely difficult to contain." Ennio looked up the stairs to where the moonlight that filtered through the high kitchen windows peeked through the cracks of the heavy door. "They are easy to hunt on a clear night with the full moon lighting both city streets and countryside as well."

"And do you have people who deal with men who become

the wolf just as you have those who follow Saverio and his undead brethren?" Evelina challenged.

"No, mia amica, mia cara, no, this night represents the sum of my involvement with any werewolf. I know first-hand of no one who has had such a meeting. I would have had help here to spare you this if I had any such assistants. My helpers do nothing but watch. You are the only one who has been there with me 'in the trenches' so to speak. My Evelina, you are the only one I trust with my whole heart."

"However," he went on in a more subdued and tentative voice, "I *have* recently discovered that the vampyres to which you refer," Ennio held his hands out in front of himself. He turned them over and back, gazing at them as if he could not believe that these hands had held a gun and used it to kill a man, a friend. He finished, "keep the werewolf population down."

Evelina eyed her childhood bulwark with distaste. With ice in her voice, she said, "You had better call your benefactor, the good doctor. We will have to commit my darling Gaetano's ruined body to the earth. Afterward, you are never, never to bother me again in this life, Ennio. Do you understand?" She stared at him for a long minute and when Ennio still did not answer, she turned to look upon the corpse of her beloved once more. She crossed herself three times, very slowly, lips moving in prayer, and then turned away.

A defeated Evelina haltingly climbed the steps away from the room about which she would have nightmares for the rest of her life. One final time, using her whole body and every ounce of strength she could muster, she pushed open the odious old door. She made her way across the lower level rooms and ascended one more flight of stairs to the sanctuary.

She pushed open an outer door and stepped into the light of the garish full moon all decked out in its gaudy, silver sequins.

She gulped in the humid summer air, trying to clear the raw scent of feral beast and the hot, metallic stench of the gun's firing from her head and lungs. She opened and closed her mouth trying to ease the ringing in her ears from the report of the gun. This initiated a coughing out of the putrid smoke emitted by the contemptible weapon. When she had recovered her breath somewhat, she started walking. She was only vaguely aware that she was moving in the direction of the building where, two days ago, she had lived as a newlywed with her adored husband.

A block from the church, before she'd even taken the turn to the long climb up the hill toward her empty home, she walked right into the arms of Saverio.

CHAPTER 21
THE RESIDUUM

Intransigent truth and solid flesh,
In a purgatory of rapturous grief
And narcosis of barbarous lust,
Offers a thunderbolt of survival.

Impacting the vampire was akin to running into a solid object and Evelina stopped in her tracks. She was too numb to be frightened or perturbed. She looked up into Saverio's green eyes. They did not look evil. His face did not have the angular, stark look of the vicious demon that lived within the man. Evelina, like a machine designed to bounce off solid objects and continue with its assignment, started to turn away. Without his seeming to move, Saverio was, again, in front of her.

"What do you want, Saverio?" Evelina spat.

"The husband, he is dead." It was a flat statement with no hint of a question about it.

"Yes, my husband is dead. Are you pleased? He is no longer an obstacle to your sick plans for me. Why don't you just get on with it?" The shattered woman raged. She had nothing to lose. She could imagine no reason to fear Saverio now. She no longer cared what he did with her. She stared defiantly into his eyes. They did not glow with sanguinary fervor. They were soft, sorrowful.

Evelina studied the creature's face. "You certainly have a full bag of tricks, Saverio," she mocked. "Don't think I believe you care about Gaetano, or even about me. I know what you are. I know how you live."

At this, the vampire reached out and gathered Evelina into his arms. With his touch, the acute tension in her shoulders released just a little. Saverio held her close to him, her head buried in his chest. He reached up with one cold hand and stroked her hair.

"It is best this way, Evelina," he asserted. She pulled back. "No, listen to me," he said as he pulled her to him again. "A vampyre has no conscience. It lives to kill without remorse. It has no feelings of empathy or sympathy for its prey. There is no guilt, only the drive to feed. But a werewolf is a beast for just one night of each moon that rises full during the nighttime hours. The rest of the time, he is human. Gaetano would have had full recall of his deeds. Any life he had would have been purgatory. Your puny man of the church can study his books until the end of time, but he will find no way to cure the disease of the wolf. Your husband was dead the instant he was scratched. It would never have been possible for you to live a lifetime keeping him contained. He would have killed. This way he never did. He leaves this earth with a conscience as clear as a baby's." He held her close, one hand on the back of her hair, the other around her narrow back. He rocked side to side a bit as if she were a child in his arms that he meant to comfort.

Evelina's heart knew that Saverio spoke the truth, but her wounds were just so raw and fresh, her grief overwhelming. Denial was her best defense. It was the only mechanism she possessed that would allow her to hold on to her anger at Ennio and fate. All the same, such a feeble means of escape was no match for Evelina's sorrow. She leaned her head back a bit to look up at Saverio. She said naught but stared into his eyes as she began to turn her head to the side exposing her long, thin neck to him in a plain invitation. When her head was turned so far that she had to look away from his face, she did speak in a small, low voice tainted with the anger that boiled within her, "Take me, Saverio. End me or make me what you are. I don't want to live with this."

A small moan escaped Saverio's lips. He wrapped her hair around the hand he held at the back of her head and leaned her head back. She felt her weakened legs give way. The creature held her upright. Just at the instant she expected to feel his pointed fangs touch her skin, he turned her, by her hair, so that they were face to face again. He did not look vampyre. He crashed his lips into hers in a rough kiss, as if to answer her anger and jolt her from her despair. Without thinking, she returned his kiss with equal hunger. She felt his tongue on her lips and encircled it with hers. All of a sudden, a picture of Gaetano lying dead on the miserable dirt floor of that putrid crypt flashed through her mind. She pulled back with all the strength left within her, shoving at Saverio's chest as she moved away from him. Saverio dropped his arms. As soon as Evelina was free of his grip she slapped his white face as hard as she could. The resulting sharp sting in her hand made Evelina gasp in the night air before straightening her body to stand as tall as she could. She wiped her lips with the back of her burning hand.

Saverio smiled benignly at her and did not follow as she brushed past him.

After a few steps, she turned. Expecting Saverio to have vanished in his usual manner, she was surprised to see him watching her go. "Saverio," she demanded, "Tell me why you come to me. Tell me why you have preserved my life for such a long time."

"Dear Evelina, my sole explanation is that I need you. I need you desperately."

"Why Saverio, why?" her attitude softened as her curiosity along with the feeling that Saverio was just another sufferer in need surfaced above her hurt and anger.

"You may be my salvation, just as you were Gaetano's. You must go now and heal. One day, when you are well, and my hour is at hand, I will come to you. I will tell you everything. Perhaps, if you care to when that day arrives, you will help me as I have helped you." Saverio finished his speech. Evelina was numb with shock. She could not, in her debilitated condition even consider the meaning of the vampire's words. They left her only more confused and tired.

"Yes, Saverio, please do come to me when you are ready. I do fear you in many ways, but I must know what your plans are for me. Now, tell me the truth. Until you are ready to reveal to me this grand and awful secret of yours, will you be watching me?"

"I will," replied Saverio with a small nod.

Evelina pulled in a deep breath and stood tall, shoulders

back, the fire of deep anger at all she had lost this night reemerging, "Then don't let me kill Ennio," she said. She turned and strode away without looking back at Saverio the vampire. Sunrise was nearing, and with the sky rapidly becoming light and clear, she knew he could not follow.

CHAPTER 22
THE ABYSS

Fevered dreams and obsessive shame
Only a cold body might quench;
A stigmata of remorse persists
For a hunger disavowed.

The days following Gaetano's death passed in a haze of grief for Evelina. Ennio's efficient acquaintance had arranged things in a satisfactory way. There were no police inquiries or questions from any quarter except Gaetano's famiglia. Evelina left all clarifications to Ennio. He dealt with loved ones, friends, and co-workers while Evelina sequestered herself in the suite of rooms with her anguish.

Ennio was the one who contacted Gaetano's employer to explain that Gaetano had died of his illness, which wasn't necessarily a lie.

Evelina chose a mahogany casket lined in white satin for its look of flawless purity in which to bury her martyred husband. His body appeared youthful and exquisitely human lying there among the lilies. He was captivatingly beautiful. It was inconceivable to the grieving bride that this was just a body, that Gaetano's essence was gone from her, never to return. Even so, Ennio conducted the Mass for the dead, and after the final graveside prayers, Gaetano was buried in the churchyard behind the place where he had been killed.

In those few days between her husband's death (or homicide as she considered it) and his funeral Mass, Evelina noticed, when they did meet in the course of the memorial preparations, that Ennio was sporting enormous dark circles under his reddened eyes. He looked as if he had spent as many hours crying as she had. She avoided any significant contact with her old compatriot speaking with him only as necessary to make Gaetano's final arrangements. She ignored the fact that the priest's uncommon self-control had been breached at last and he was clearly suffering.

There was no sign of the infectious, mad cousin at Gaetano's wake. Evelina learned that the poor woman was now also dead. She had passed in her sleep, Gaetano's aunt told her, not long after the star-crossed wedding. "We did not want to burden you and poor Gaetano with the knowledge of such a sad event while you were in your newlywed bliss," said the woman, as she burst into tears. She clutched Evelina in a long, swaying hug. Evelina patted the woman and whispered comfort to her, wondering how much more she could take of this devastating, cruel day. But the new widow conversely felt no small amount of relief knowing that no one else would lose his life, or her sanity, because of the tainted blood of the young woman. *So much wasted life and love*, Evelina lamented as she dropped a fresh tear on the back of the other bereaved woman's black dress.

Gaetano's parents and his two younger brothers were Evelina's biggest social obstacles on the awful day of her husband's burial. She had left every detail of the version of events they would present to her husband's mourners to Ennio. She knew that she could not look her husband's closest relatives in the eye and lie to them about their loved one's passing. She adored Gaetano's people. She wondered if they, who had become her family through her marriage would now drift away from her. She was broken by her own grief but did her best to offer whatever solace she could to the people who raised her lost love and to those who had grown up with him. The most distressing part of the awful day came as his mother implored Evelina with pleading eyes, "Did my son suffer terribly?"

The kindest thing that Evelina could think to say, without lying outright, was, "Not for long, Darling."

Once she had finished accepting the sympathy of Gaetano's co-workers, Evelina left the church. She had refused all offers to come and stay with Gaetano's relatives, or the nuns at St. Catherine's for the time being. She returned to her quiet flat without a word to Ennio. He had watched her go. As she passed by him, she looked into his face and saw pain and pleading that she could not and would not answer. She didn't care about his sorrow. He was a murderer in her view, and she planned to shun him for the rest of her life.

Evelina's anger sustained her through the following months. She passed much of her time resting and recovering from the long, terrifying few days during which she had lost so much blood and watched her husband transform into a demon hound. She doubted that any amount of time, no matter how tranquil, could erase the horror of seeing Gaetano be shot to death, or of witnessing his body be laid to rest decades before it would have grown old and declined in a natural way.

It was a slow recovery filled with melancholy days and nightmares when she was able to sleep. In time, though, she was able to eat and regain a bit of strength. Once she could concentrate enough to make sense of words on a page, she spent a good portion of each day studying the subject of vampyre lore in anticipation of Saverio's promise. Her attempts frustrated her because most of the material she found approached the subject as if it were myth when she knew first hand that the demon undead lived and walked among human beings. She knew that Ennio had access to texts that were more factual, practical, and informative. Though she coveted his connections, Evelina stubbornly refused to contact the rector.

At some point, with the help of sweet Sister Agnese from St Catherine's, she packed away Gaetano's clothing and personal belongings. The residence became as it had been before she met her ill-fated beloved: a singular and more feminine environment. She had never even gotten the chance to display photos of her wedding day. Now that prospect was much too painful.

Each day she slept some, she ate when she felt the need, she prayed feverishly, and she brooded. Her heart continued to grieve for her murdered husband, but her head was filled with Saverio. She wondered every day if the vampire specter was near. She often felt he might be, but she was never certain. She would be walking from the market or the bookshop, and the fine hairs on the back of her neck would stand up. A tingling would travel up her spine and when it reached her head her body would quiver once from top to bottom. Even though she would often detect movement in her periphery, there was nothing when she turned her head. She told herself that there could be any number of explanations for the unsettling sensations she was experiencing. It was easy and logical to credit her distraction to the persistence of her depleted, vulnerable condition and her grief.

She contemplated her situation over and over again. Did she have a spectral hunter or did she not? If she did, what could she do about it? Maybe she should call la policia to report that a man was following her and watching her. No, no, she would reason, because she could not see him. He could evaporate at will. A human constable would have very little luck apprehending him. She could imagine how seriously her report of being stalked by an invisible fiend would be taken! And did she, perhaps, wish to be followed? Was she safer with Saverio about? Without question, her desire to know the meaning behind the cryptic words the vampire had spoken on the night of Gaetano's demise had not waned. Would he return to her as he had promised? It was a roundabout of questions that never ceased.

Evelina had disturbing thoughts of Saverio beyond worry concerning his whereabouts. Over and over she surrendered herself to provocative, sensual daydreams for which she roundly chastised herself. She couldn't stop remembering the way it felt in the vampire's arms. Again and again, she recalled his wintry touch on her hot skin. She remembered his kisses, both the sweet and gentle, and the deep and searching. She reminded herself time and again that Saverio was a monstrous bully with destructive intent. What kind of a woman was she that she welcomed his caresses? She tried to remember that vampyres had the power to bewitch, to entice. They possessed the ability to make one feel desire when one should feel revulsion. But Saverio wasn't there hypnotizing her as she tossed and turned, her skin burning the white sheets even on the coldest nights. Tears drenched her pillow as she remembered each detail of her enigmatic shadow. She longed for him even as she continued to mourn her sweet husband. *Was she not a grieving widow? Mesmeric spells aside, how could she dream of another man, especially one so evil?* Guilt ravaged her psyche because she could not banish Saverio from her mind. She prayed for release from the spell she was under. She prayed for the vision of his searing green eyes to leave her.

Some days Evelina envied Gaetano his peace. He was out of all this now, and safe with his God. She recited rosary after rosary, petitioning the Blessed Virgin for Her intercession. The seasons passed.

CHAPTER 23
THE INVOCATION

Obsidian mist descends
Upon the ivory effigy
Bringing with it an entreaty
For fatal absolution.

S pring came again to Evelina's world with a profusion of blooms, sweetly-scented air, and a period of seductively clement weather. Her unbearable and stabbing, wretched grief had ebbed to a dull aching fog as the months passed. On the other hand, her obsessive imaginings of Saverio increased in frequency and intensity. Her studies had revealed to her horrifying truths about the night-stalking breed of entity with which she was infatuated. These realities aside, Saverio continued to haunt her dreams and her every waking thought. *It is my way of dealing with my loss*, she continued to tell herself.

Evelina had not met Saverio, or even sensed him since the

tourists had begun to return in force to the city. She wandered for hours through the streets hoping he would fulfill his promise and come to her, whether it would spell disaster or hope for her life, for her future. She wondered if perhaps he had moved on and left her alone at last. Instead of the relief she had always assumed his departure would bring, she felt more loss, more sadness.

She refused to seek out Ennio. She attended Mass in her own parish, though she often visited Gaetano's grave. She covered the site with plantings. Hours drifted by as she tended the flowering plants and talked to the husband she had lost, begging his forgiveness for letting him die so young and in such a horrible way. She confessed her obsession with Saverio and implored Gaetano's spirit to help her, if somehow it was able, to banish her disturbing thoughts and end her obsession.

Ennio came to the churchyard to try to talk with Evelina several times. He inquired about her days and offered unwanted advice. He recommended that she move from her lonely home with its sad memories. It outraged her that he would think she could ever leave the home she had shared with her family, and ever so fleetingly, her Gaetano. She told him to mind his own business and leave her be, and he eventually gave up his entreaties. Evelina did not explain to the worried cleric or admit to herself that she would not leave her home because waiting for Saverio to return to her was the thing that made her want to continue to draw breath. Whatever the entity wanted from her, she needed to be certain that she could be found when he was ready to reveal himself.

And then, one day in early May, Evelina returned from a

renewing visit to the orphanage and found the front door, that was less than a year old standing open. A scent like heaven wafted into the hallway. When she peeked into her rooms, her heart racing with anticipation, she saw that branches of lavender lilacs had been made into a huge bouquet and placed on the white Carrara of her kitchen countertop. The profusion of flowers was irresistible to her. She walked straight to them and buried her face in the blooms without stopping to think about from where they had come, or of who might be inside.

Seconds later, Evelina felt a movement. She perceived a presence behind her. Verging on intoxication from the scent of the multitudinous blooms, she froze with her face leaning into the blossoms. Bitter words rose in her throat for Ennio with his peace offering. She would call the portiere up from the lobby and have the persistent clergyman thrown out. She started to turn, but cool hands touched her shoulders and held her facing away from their owner. She knew now that it was Saverio. He was close enough that she was able to inhale the spicy scent of him along with the overwhelming fragrance of the lilacs. It made her feel light-headed.

"I have seen you stop to breathe in the perfume of these flowers often, my Evelina," her vampire tenderly blew the words into her ear.

With tears forming in her dark brown eyes, she whispered, "Saverio, it *is* you."

He turned her around to face him. She caught her breath at his pale beauty. His green eyes were softer than she remembered them. They were not just softer. They were different somehow, more unguarded. He bent low over her and whispered, "My time is at hand, Evelina. I need you badly. Answer me this. Are you afraid?"

"No, Saverio, I no longer fear you. I feel I *should* be afraid, yet I am not. I know that you have the mastery to control my responses. Your venom has stunned me as Ennio has told me over and over again. About this, I no longer care. He says that you can't feel; that you can't be kind. Yet I want to know you. I want to know everything." She lowered her eyes as she elaborated, "My feelings may be false, but I can't resist them. I can't resist *you*."

Saverio made a low snarling sound and then exploded. "That little weasel of a priest! He preaches far too much. He thinks he knows all. He knows nothing!" He lifted Evelina's chin with one white hand and looked into her eyes. His tone softened as he explained, "Ennio is talking about a cheap vampyre's trick employed to make people their victims. I have never employed such a device with you, Evelina. I never will." Saverio interrupted his tirade as he dropped his hand from her face, held her by both arms again, and looked away. He seemed to be considering something. After a few seconds, he looked back to her and demanded, "Just when did our friend, the ordained one, tell you these things about me?"

Evelina reflected for a short while and then responded, "Well, he cautioned me about your power to entrance after the night I first saw you. Her tender eyes filled as she went on, "The night Annabella was massacred by those barbarians." She wiped at one eye with the back of her hand, gathered in her sorrow, and went on, "He has repeated his warnings to me about you again and again over the years. He did so when I returned from," she faltered before finishing, "Paris."

"But not since the death of your husband." It was a

statement, not a question. "And do you think that Ennio would have let me come here tonight if he continued to believe that?"

This night was the first time Evelina could remember Saverio calling Ennio by his given name. He had done it twice now, after initially cursing his old nemesis. She rationalized, "You may have made yourself unseen by Ennio and his minions.

"You well know that Ennio and I aren't the intimates we once were. The urge to punish him may have passed but we don't speak often," she said with her chin lifted in a defiant gesture. "The truth is that I have insisted he leave me alone. I don't need him or want him in my life."

Saverio laughed softly, "No, of course you don't," he said. "And I'm sure Ennio has forgotten all about you by now." His smirk made his sarcasm clear to Evelina. She frowned in annoyance and turned her head from Saverio in defiance of his gentle taunts.

As had become the norm of late, when she let herself think about Ennio, Evelina was stabbed with guilt for having abandoned her old benefactor. She, who loved everyone with a mother's love, independent of what they did to hurt her, knew that Ennio was suffering. Her heart and her conscience ached to think that her words and actions contributed to his misery. But, inasmuch as she knew that Gaetano was already doomed when it happened, Ennio had slain her husband. While Evelina was almost unfailingly empathetic and often kind to her detriment, she was not entirely immune to selfish human impulses. She needed to blame someone for the unspeakable thing that had happened to her innocent husband and the loss of the serene life she had anticipated. In the depths of her being, she was aware that the guilt she carried for her attraction to Saverio was another reason she clung to the circumstances of Gaetano's demise and Ennio's part in it. She held these things before her like a shield against her raw humanity. But the truth was that she missed Ennio. Her failure to comfort him in what was, for him too, a time of grief and mourning overflowed the sea of her guilt. For all that, she persisted in her unwillingness to yield to her feelings. She was not ready to admit to them.

Once again Saverio caught her chin, guiding her eyes back to his with a gentle movement. His smile was gone now. He spoke with a low fervor that made Evelina's skin vibrate. "Whatever you feel about me, my beguiling Evelina, it is real. It comes from your loving and generous heart. Yours is the kindest heart I have ever chanced to encounter. You have asked me 'why' many times. Why have I sought you out? Why have I protected you? This is why Evelina. You are the one person I have found in a century of searching whose heart possesses love enough to save me. I am experiencing the human condition once again." He brought his face closer to hers. "I, too, feel empathy and sympathy and desire. I yearn for human connection, for love. The bittersweet pangs of it are overwhelming," he whispered. "Evelina," he finished, "I am in dire need of a savior."

When he was done speaking, Evelina placed her head on his quiet chest. The exotic redolence of him mixed, again, with the flowers. It was lilacs, cinnamon, and patchouli, the scent and the joy of every season combined. It was life. The irony of it did not escape her. She put her arms around Saverio, drinking in his essence for a long moment. Then, ever polite and considerate, she said, "Saverio, please come and sit down. Won't you let me take your coat? It is quite warm."

He pulled the coat off, and Evelina could see that, although he was thin, the muscles of his chest and arms made iron ripples under the black silk shirt he wore. The pair sat down beside each other on the blush leather. Evelina reached out to take Saverio's chill, but not icy, pale hands in hers. "I have long felt something for you, Saverio. I knew that I was supposed to be repulsed by you, but I was not. Even on that first night, I was drawn to you. I was terrified of you for many years. I was most frantic when I could see the demon within you come out, as it did the night you went after those devils who butchered sweet Annabella. But no matter how frightened I was or how sinful I believed myself to be, I was always attracted to you. Now you are telling me that I am a good, kind person and you want my help even though I have been fascinated by a," she hesitated, "killer, all these years?"

"Yes, beautiful Evelina, you have enough compassion within to care even for a killer," whispered Saverio. "Let go of your shame."

Evelina had always believed, and Ennio had confirmed, that her inability to resist Saverio during their few intimate meetings was not because of anything genuine within her. It was because she was under some type of glamour. It was disconcerting to her to imagine that she had felt a natural desire for Saverio, even on the day she married Gaetano. Admitting to herself that some part of her had always wanted Saverio, she had a reflexive thought that she should get to confession as soon as possible.

What was more, despite her protestations to Saverio, she knew that Ennio would never abandon her.

It made her drop her guard, and her self-reproach for just an instant and smile to admit both of these truths to herself. Saverio responded with the smallest of smiles of his own as he pulled Evelina to him. All pretense of visitor's etiquette or of resistance fell away as Evelina lifted her face to Saverio's. Their lips came together. His were smooth and firm. He moved them hungrily over Evelina's mouth. She shifted closer into his rock-hard body and pressed herself to him. He moved his lips and his teeth, sharp but not piercing, over her face and then lower over her throat. Evelina's breath came in panting bursts. Her arms were around the vampire's neck. She lifted one hand to the back of his head and pulled him closer still. "I love you, Saverio," she whispered into his ear, "I have loved you for so long."

He replied with a long, low, and primitive moan. "Evelina, my darling," he was able to say, "I feel we have loved each other for millennia."

"Yes," she whispered, "It is as if, perhaps, lifetime after lifetime we have come together and been wrenched apart. The ache of it is almost more than I can bear. But the joy, mio Saverio, it is exquisite!" Saverio emitted a choked gasp; almost a sob.

They made love there on the sofa, their passion so intense, so all- engrossing that the night passed by without Evelina noticing the moment Saverio began to breathe. Only as the midnight hours waned, and a spent Evelina lay with her head on Saverio's lean, solid chest did she realize that it was moving with air. She felt his breath in her hair as she watched his rib cage rise and collapse, moving her head and shoulders ever so subtly up and down, up and down. When she carefully turned, placing her ear on the appropriate spot, she heard the faint beating of a heart within Saverio's centuries-old body.

She listened to the faint thump, thumping of her no longer undead amante's ancient heart for a long minute. And then she lifted her head to find his eyes with hers. "Saverio?" she encouraged.

"Yes, I feel the need to breathe at times," he confirmed. "We have much to talk about, Evelina. I can't leave now. The sun is coming up, and I remain unable to tolerate full sun," he said.

She prompted, "But you will be able to?"

"Perhaps, my love, perhaps," he affirmed.

CHAPTER 24
THE CRUCIATION

To butcher with abandon,
Bloodless bodies strewn about?
To terrorize and crucify, dishonor burning white,
Or to face an eternal penalty of the adversary's feast?

Evelina slipped from Saverio's arms as he slept. She stood and crossed the room so that she could close the shades against the light lest it burn her lover's pale body uncovered as it was in all its awful, immortal beauty. She took a moment to admire him and wonder at his musculature, his form, and the mystery of his existence before returning to lie beside her inamorato on the cushiony sofa. Saverio pulled her to him. He kissed her long and with extraordinary tenderness. They made love once again in the filtered light of the warm room.

They had been drowsing, their bodies tangled together, for just a short while when Saverio let out a legitimate, long sigh. He rose to a sitting position and scooped Evelina into his arms. He sat her next to him as if she were made of fragile porcelain and said, "Mia carissima, we must talk."

Evelina nodded. She stood and went into the bedroom. When she returned, she was wearing a lavender wrapper and carrying a quilted throw. She had intended to offer the coverlet to Saverio, but the newly human man had slipped back into his pants and loose, black shirt. He was standing somewhat awkwardly in the middle of the room, his bare feet strikingly white against his black pants. Evelina noticed that, conversely, his face was not as starkly pale as she was used to seeing it. A slight flush of pink had shown itself just below his prominent cheekbones.

Evelina seated herself back on the sofa, patting the cushion beside her. She said, "Tell me, Saverio."

And he would. He would tell her of his long, unholy, horrible existence. She would be appalled, but not surprised because she had known it would be as he said.

The vampire Saverio began. "Evelina, do you remember when I explained to you that Gaetano would be doomed to live with his guilt if he killed?"

She looked at her lap. "Yes, I do indeed remember. I may not have taken your words to heart when you first spoke them, but I do remember. Not a day has gone by since without my thinking of them."

Holding her eyes with his, he stated, "It is coming to that for me."

"Oh, my Saverio," moaned Evelina.

"No, my love, let me go on. You must understand, and it is a difficult tale to unfold to you because your part in it will not be easy," Saverio warned.

Evelina nodded as she tried to adjust her expression into one of studious interest, even as her mind spun with questions.

Saverio set his story in motion, "No other of my kind has lived as long as I. A vampyre is not, in truth, an immortal being. It can be exterminated. That is what happens to most of us sooner or later, for all that, the monster within us makes every brutal effort to survive as long as it can."

Evelina's eyes widened. A tremor rushed through her. Saverio went on. "While we almost never as vampires, seek death, it is a godsend when it comes. And it is not just salvation for the many who will not become our victims. It is a blessing for the monster itself, or shall we say the host of the monster, because if we live long enough, our buried humanity returns. It squirms and claws its way back to us. The racking pain of this process weakens the body but it strengthens the revenant. The corrupt spirit that inhabits our earthly form tires. It weakens and recedes. We can summon it if we choose. However, we choose to do so less and less often. At this stage of being, we begin to age as a human once more. We again know hunger and pain. The worst of it is that we endure the most abominable, shattering guilt. We think back upon our deeds and the terror and anguish they have caused, and we are in insufferable agony."

"No, it can't be," said Evelina. "Do you mean to say that this thing that is happening to you means that you will, someday, lose your human life all over again?"

"If a body is invaded by the vampyre spirit soon enough after the life has left it, that human death does not stand for eternity. This was true for me," confirmed Saverio. "Our human soul, asleep in the ether for century after century, awakens and asserts itself. It instigates a monumental war against the invading entity. While time itself begins the process, I have come to believe that this growth of the soul originates with the help of a chance catalyst, or one sent by a merciful god perhaps. I know that my humanity awakened when I first saw you, my beloved Evelina.

Evelina's heart brimmed with hope. She pulled her torso up straight and exclaimed, "Then you can have a real life in the sun again! You can grow old and die peacefully in your bed."

Saverio shook his head, closing his eyes as if in acute discomfort, "Please let me finish, Evelina, before you make any plans for me," he pleaded.

"Go on, Saverio," Evelina whispered.

"I must still feed in order to live, although I believe that need would subside if I went on long enough," he continued.

Evelina shuddered again at the prospect but bravely coaxed, "And upon whom do you feed, Saverio?"

"Those who would impart evil by their wish or by their curse," he answered.

Understanding dawned. "Gaetano's cousin?" Evelina inquired.

Saverio did not look away. "Yes, I drained her of her blood. I sent the unfortunate woman to her grave so that no more would be infected with her disease and she would suffer no longer." He spoke without apology or subterfuge.

"I am very glad that you did that, my love," Evelina admitted.

Saverio paused, studying Evelina's face. She thought he looked surprised by her approval. He went on, "There are many stories of those I have killed. Many of them had done much damage to others and the world. I have been their judge, their jury, and their executioner. I play God because of my own base needs. It isn't noble, and it only adds to my guilt."

He sighed with his halting voice, once, and then took a slow, deliberate breath. It was a deeper and more even breath than Evelina had yet heard emanate from her vampire lover. "Let me tell you now a centuries-old story," he began.

Evelina wrapped her two hands through Saverio's arm as if to hold him up and console him as he persevered with his chronicle. "Go on, my love," she encouraged. Saverio did.

CHAPTER 25
THE ANCIENTS

The shocking carnage of the glaive
With its dire expanse of rotting enemies
And the odious pecking of crows,
Exposes the grievous sins of the damned.

"Tepes, the Dragon, lived for five hundred years as a vampire before his humanity rose to the surface. After five centuries of possession, the demon Drago was so formidable that only with his consent could he be slain. He languished in a sea of madness for almost another one hundred years before, in a rare burst of clarity, he begged to die, and he was given release." Saverio placed his head in his hands.

"He was released by you," Evelina stated.

Saverio looked up. "Yes, he made me what I am. We fought as soldiers, side by side. We killed together in life and we butchered our enemies together in death. In the end, I watched him weaken, and I finished him. I put a stake of wood through his antiquated but still-beating heart. I sliced off his head with a dull sword. I cut his heart out of his withered chest and buried it far from the rest of his useless body. I felt nothing as I did these deeds but a remnant of loyalty from our shared years. My body and soul were dominated by the vampyre demon at that point in time, and I was incapable of genuine compassion."

Insofar as she had been prepared by Ennio's research, hearing these details in Saverio's own words, in his voice, was disquieting for Evelina. At the imagery his drama evoked, and with the growing horror of her full understanding, Evelina grew pale. The storyteller, seeing her distress, placed a bracing hand on her forehead. She would have liked to stay just that way for hours, but Saverio stood. He went to the kitchen and ran her a glass of water. He handed the drink to her as he sat back down beside her. She drained the glass, and then looked back to the mysterious man beside her.

"He created you," Evelina echoed Saverio's revelation. "You are that much older now than he was when you, well, ended his ordeal. You lived in his age and were a soldier! Oh, Saverio, is that the only life you knew? Did you love, did you marry?"

"No, Darling, I knew just the crusade, with the exception of my ephemeral childhood. I am descended from the Veneti people. My ancestors lived in Venice. It was the crusades that drove them eastward. Some fought, some fled. When I was a child, la mia famiglia lived in a small cottage on the border of what was then called Walachia near the Danube. I remember my father as a kind, peaceful man. I don't know if he ever had been a warrior. My mother was pure love. I recall her singing in a low, sweet voice. I tried always to be on hand when she washed her long, chestnut hair. It was spectacular! My baby sisters were glorious; innocence personified. They were such jolly children. I did know love in those days; love, satisfying work, and contentment."

Saverio became quiet, seeming to be lost in his memories. Evelina encouraged, "I hope you will tell me more about your people one day, Saverio."

"We shall see, mia dolce Evelina," Saverio, awakened now from his reverie. "When there is time. Time," he murmured.

"My parents and all of my siblings were massacred by the Turks when I was just a boy." Evelina gasped but Saverio went on. "I was the sole member of my small clan to escape. This fact alone, by the way, provides enough guilt for any man to endure!" Saverio hung his head once again. He made a low choking noise. Evelina placed her water glass on the blonde end table beside her. She wrapped her arms around Saverio, squeezing him to her for another long minute before he gingerly pulled away from her hold.

"Are you ready to go on, love?" queried Evelina. "I am here, darling; I am here," she added.

Saverio nodded. He sat up straight to continue with his soliloquy. "Our surname was Tanicani and, for me at least, it was prophetic. It means he who comes in the night. I lived a life of fighting in the night and later endured death hunting in the night. I fought for some years alongside those who had rescued me.

These men, and more women than you may imagine, belonged to the Order of the Dragon. One of them grabbed me and dragged me away from my home as the band fought off the Turks who had just annihilated my loved ones for nothing but the bit of food we had on hand in our small cottage. Robbery was only a pretext for them, of course. They killed by dint of pure bloodlust.

The man who pulled me away from the carnage in my boyhood home was Vladimir Tepes a Sárkány. I came to know him as simply Drago. He, with a few of his closest cohorts, were searching for Turk invaders that had escaped a nearby battle when they heard the screams of my family. Drago and his men ran off the trespassers, killing several of them. The fierce leader impaled one soldier on the man's own sword. I later learned that there was a reason it was not enough for some enemies to be run through with a sword or bashed in the head. When one is expecting to meet the eyes of another frightened young soldier approaching from the other side of a shadowy battlefield but, instead, is confronted with the visage of a miscreant with bared fangs, one understands."

He paused for a moment. "Just as you understand, poor Evelina, knowing that image as you do," he acknowledged before continuing his saga. "Many a vampyre has found its way to an army where it can sate its thirst for blood alongside the supposed righteous who fight for good. A great many soldiers were impaled by the infamous and horrible Tepes to disguise vampyre executions. Who would come to fight, if the fight were against devils rather than mere men? He did what had to be done. But his actions became more and more obscene over the years. He was a brutal warrior who grew to believe that the blood of his enemies made him strong. Taking a page from the vampyres' book, he drank from his enemies. He even bathed in their blood."

Evelina cringed. Her face burned. She lifted Saverio's hand

to her cheek for the coolness of it as she worked to keep down the bile that rose in her throat.

"This was the nature of our sorry, violent lives," Saverio pushed on, "until the day the Impaler was wounded. Even as he fell, several vampiric beings surrounded him and, taking advantage of his weakness, fed from him en masse. I was beside him in the battle. I attempted to fight off the devils, but they threw me aside as if I were made of air. The Dragon was renowned and powerful. It was he they were after. I fell to my hands and knees just a short way from the scene of the savages slurping away on the lifeblood of my leader. I vomited, even though the scene was no more abhorrent than much of what I witnessed each day on those medieval battlefields. I knew that what was coming for me was not a swift and noble death. I wanted to get up and fall on my weapon to avoid my commander's demonic assailants and the vampyre curse, but I was weak with sickness, frozen with fear. I looked up from my heaving to see one of the fiends open its wrist with the sword of Drago himself. The thing dripped its flowing blood over the lips of the fallen warrior's body. And then, to my horror, I witnessed the man beside whom I had long fought, so unmistakably dead, stir, and begin to drink hungrily from the devil's open vein. When the Dragon was sated, he turned his head to look in my direction. His eyes glowed yellow. I wanted to run, but I could not look away from those hideous burning eyes."

Evelina was awed by the apex of Saverio's saga of his ancient mentor. She sat transfixed; her eyes as wide as a child's.

Saverio focused on the air over Evelina's shoulder as he told the next part of his gruesome epic.

"As the great warrior rose from the patch of earth where he had died, the devils who had attacked him scattered. It was as if they intuited that he was already more powerful, more dangerous than they would ever be. My mentor approached me. I could not drop my eyes from his."

"'Stand,'" he ordered when he grew close to where I knelt with my face locked onto those glowing eyes."

"I did, of course," sighed Saverio. "But something came over me. I remembered my long-dead gente. It was enough to remind me to pray to the God for which I fought. I was able to break the Dragon's stare. I ran. But no mere man can outrun a powerful immortal, and Drago's command was immense right from the inception of his vampiric life. He manifested in my path, locking those poisonous eyes on me once again. Centuries later I can still recall the pain of my head being violently wrenched to the side and the fiery puncture of Drago's new vampyre fangs."

Here Saverio gave a sharp, humorless laugh. He said, "I suppose he must have gloried in the ease of using his teeth to drain his victims after all the years he had to open their veins with his sword to collect their blood in his hands."

Saverio's rendition seemed to Evelina to have no end, and she wished that it *could* end because she knew what was coming next. He pushed ahead even as her whole body quaked beside him. "Drago's wounds were healing preternaturally quickly, but he continued to bleed from his throat. He forced my face to the gash. I tried to resist. I tasted his blood and tried to spit it away. Drago grabbed my hair and jerked my head back. He fixed his demonic stare hard upon me. I grew calm as my human essence drained from my body. The demon pulled my face back to his throat, and, bewitched, I drank. I had prayed to my God for death. Instead, compelled by those glowing yellow eyes, I became a monster.

"Oh," said Evelina. "Oh, no."

Saverio looked up at her and said, "I am sorry mia vita. I should not be telling you all of this in such grisly detail."

Evelina was shaking her head. "No, no, I want to hear every particular, Saverio," she reassured him. "But perhaps some more water?" she suggested, holding up her empty glass.

When Saverio returned with the full, chilled glass, Evelina took it and placed it to her temple for a second or two before taking another long drink. "I am ready, Saverio, go on."

"Are you certain, my love?"

Evelina sat up a bit straighter. "If I am to be of any help to you, Saverio, I should know everything. Yes, finish your story, Darling. Please."

Saverio offered her a sad smile and a lift of his brow in apology. Then he proceeded with his dark and tragic narration. "After my attack," he picked up his chronicle, "I dreamed of the loved ones that had been gone from me for so many years. But in the dream, I felt nothing for them. I awoke to a brutish hunger for blood. I had never before drank from that of my enemies as Vladimir the Dragon had done in life. Now, I was pure demon and needed blood just as you needed that draught of water. I stalked, and I killed. I drank the blood from the young and the old, the good and the hateful. I drank from humans whenever I was able. I drank from small wildlife and city vermin when I needed to.

The men who found me the day my family was slaughtered had taken me with them and taught me to fight and to kill my enemies. When my mentor turned demon that day, he set about creating his new army. I was his first initiate. For hundreds of years, I brutally drained the blood of guiltless victims by his side, without remorse."

Evelina was shaken. She held back tears. She had known that Saverio had been, was, a killer. The carnage for which he had been responsible over the centuries was horrifying. For all that, it was the tale of the innocent child he had once been having been coerced into a life of war and death that was most heartbreaking to her.

"To answer the question you posed when I began this morbid drama, Evelina," Saverio disclosed in a hushed tone, "no, I never knew love of any kind after the day la mia famiglia was killed until the night your sweet classmate was slain and I held you in my arms."

Evelina closed her eyes and exhaled the breath she had been holding. She thrilled to know that Saverio had loved her from the moment of their first touch.

Her flush of excitement at Saverio's profession was short-lived. She could not recall that fateful night without thinking of Annabella's awful death. Further, she was saddened to the core by what she had learned of Saverio's lost family and the horrors of his long, long life.

She rested her eyes as she waited for him to continue. As upsetting as were Saverio's reminiscences, she had waited for an age, it seemed, to hear this legend and she would not shy away from the awful story now. She had declared to her amante that she must hear the account in its entirety, and she would.

"I have never been far from you since that night," Saverio pushed forward. "I first saw you, Evelina, and your Ennio, through the iron fence of your primary school when you were a delicate, blossoming child."

Evelina gasped and opened her eyes. "You have known me that long, my love?" Evelina was astounded!

"Oh, yes," Saverio went on, "Changes were initiated within me many years before the night of Annabella's demise."

"Soon after I felt the first stirrings of humanity within me, I set out to make my way back from the east to Italia. I remembered that Venice was the home of my people so I reasoned that I should return there. I found little there to tempt me. I had become averse to the hunt and the only thing other than humanity Venice had to offer was the damp. I was a lost and desperate animal. One night as I prepared to make a victim, a meal, of a stunning young man not so different from your Gaetano, I looked into his eyes and saw a person, a life. I left the man without tasting his blood and dined on rats for days afterward. I had begun to see humans as souls rather than prey. I could distinguish the difference between good and evil. I was drawn more and more to good but not in the old way. I did not want to feed upon the virtuous, the pure; I wanted only to be near them. I struck out for the holy city seeking my new sustenance, righteousness. If I didn't find it there, I would at least, I supposed, find dry underground accommodations."

"Once in Rome, I found that it was no more or less holy than any other place, but I felt as if I were home," Saverio's tale progressed. "There was something here for me, I knew. I like to think it was God's mercy leading me to you, bellissima Evelina."

Evelina smiled and touched the vampire's cheek.

Saverio carried on. "I would pass schoolyards just to feel

the innocence of the children there. I wondered at how that innocence no longer incited me to brutal murder. Instead, it touched a sweet but painful something within me."

"I do remember what I said at your wedding celebration, mia amore. I goaded Ennio, and you, too, by threatening the children in attendance. By the day of your wedding, it had been decades since I had fed on the pure of heart." Saverio looked past Evelina, his eyes far away. She felt his regret and guilt but she let it be.

"I found I could even produce tears, as I had not for centuries." Saverio's voice broke. "I could think of those I had loved, dead for more than five hundred years and mourn the loss of them once again."

"And then one day I noted something else; a masterful kindness, that is, a kindness filled with power. I sought this power. I found it to be emanating from a wee dark-haired girl with big, innocent brown eyes and her small helpmate. They were just burying a dead sparrow under a tree at the edge of the school playground, but the vibrations of love emanating from them were breathtaking." Saverio studied Evelina's face as he spoke of the day that he had found her.

"That first day I saw you and felt the strength of your faith, the grace that flowed from you almost brought me to my knees just as the force of Drago's licentiousness had."

Evelina was too fascinated with Saverio's declaration to be nonplussed by his praise. She said nothing but gave a small shake of her head as if to deny her goodness.

Saverio went on, "I let myself be drawn to your power and virtue again and again as you grew. I assigned myself your safeguard. I knew that there was a potential within you that must be preserved, a virtue that might even deliver me from my living hell one day. Other demons are drawn to the good and the strong though they more often make prey of the frail. When these monsters seek the good, it is with evil intent. I did all that I could to keep you and yours safe." He faltered before adding, "I wasn't able to save your parents. Even a vampyre cannot sense a tragic accident coming. I am desperately sorry that I could not."

With a sad smile for her companion, Evelina said, "Of course you could not, darling. I had a premonition of the disaster myself and have always felt I should somehow have convinced Mama and Papa not to board that plane. That is my cross to bear, not yours, Saverio."

It was the vampire's turn to shake his head in denial. He took Evelina's two hands in his and brought his forehead to hers. "No, Evelina, let go of that burden. Would you hold another hostage to such a thing? Would you place that cross upon another young girl's shoulders? We both know that you would not, and you must not do such a thing to yourself."

Saverio lifted his head to look into Evelina's misting eyes.

"The night Annabella was killed I did fail. I failed miserably." There was real anguish in Saverio's voice. "I mourned your precious friend and still accuse myself of her death with every sunset. But I could only defend one of you from the malicious predators in that alleyway, you see."

"I should have sensed their evil intent myself," protested Evelina.

"No, Evelina, no, you could not because those creatures had no souls. It was I who knew and I who betrayed my duty." Saverio pleaded with Evelina with his malachite eyes for forgiveness. She gave it with a slow, measured kiss for each side of his cool, smooth face.

But the rest of his confession could not wait. Saverio's next words tumbled out of him and they were filled with fire. "When I held you, I knew that it was true. You had enough love and enough faith to rescue even me. After that night, insulating you from danger became much more than a compulsion. It was more than instinct or my selfish hope of salvation that drew me to you. I was able to feel real love, human love coming from my ravaged heart. I loved you, Evelina, with all of it. Contrarily, the devil that persisted within me had no ability to express that love. It despised Gaetano. I think my human self hated him as well, but I would have saved him from his trial had I been able to pinpoint the source of the threat and subdue it sooner. It shames me to admit my loathing for your fated husband. He was a good man. You very much deserve to have any man you chose to share in your life be a good man. Yet, Evelina, I have considered you mine since that first night. My emerging mortal jealousy tangled together with a demon's rage at Gaetano for having you by his side and in his bed. This was a new kind of torment for me."

You were no longer that tiny schoolyard saint, but a woman. My demon self had lived long but my human mind and body were young. I was in love with you and I wanted you; I was hungry for your attention, your touch."

Evelina thrilled at his words. Her whole body vibrated.

"These feelings were within me well before Gaetano's curse," Saverio continued. "I smelled the wolf on him as I followed you in Paris, and I vowed that I would not let the full moon rise without protecting you."

"If you wonder, mia cara, I do know what a twisted thing is a stalking mutant who is obsessed with you, in love with you." Saverio avoided Evelina's eyes as he confessed his shame.

"Yes," Evelina responded, his confession bringing her back to the present moment. "It should be unthinkable even to sit here in my living room with a man who surreptitiously trailed me across a continent. I could never have imagined before you came into my life, that I would be so profoundly intimate with a man I once feared might harm me. Had I not learned that you have been my benevolent guardian I would be mortally ashamed of my flagrant self-destructiveness. Why did you never before let me know that it was not the evil spirit in you that was taunting me, Saverio?"

She could barely hear his answer, "Because, my love, often it was."

Evelina shuddered. She swallowed hard but did not speak. She was afraid to ask anything more about Saverio's past intentions.

When Saverio picked up his narrative in a calmer manner, he again changed course.

"You can't have known this, but I hovered nearby on the awful night of your husband's transformation, my sweet Evelina."

She was taken aback by Saverio's announcement. "You were near? How near, Saverio? I did not see you until I left..." she paused, "that place."

"On the night of your husband's metamorphosis," explained Saverio, "I still possessed, very nearly, the full powers of the incorporeal. I was there in that horrid dungeon with you, the wolf, and the fumbling padre. My physical being was no more than mist, but I was there. I was ready to incarnate if need be.

"Why didn't you do that, Saverio," Evelina prompted.

Saverio looked into Evelina's eyes. "I did not want to be the one to end him. I did not want you to see me wound him. I could not bear to have you detest me for his destruction."

"Oh, Saverio, mio Saverio," whispered a tearful Evelina.

CHAPTER 26

THE ANOINTING

Wantonly desperate communion,
An affirmation of existence,
Is poisoned by the umbra
Of crouching, lethal reality.

They sat there, not touching, for a long minute. Evelina excused herself. After a short stay in the toilette, she emerged, face damp, hair combed into soft waves about her face. When she was seated next to him again, Saverio picked up his recitation, carrying it in yet another new direction and one Evelina had not anticipated.

"Do you know of Stoker and his myths?"

"Yes, I do," said Evelina as she settled herself back on the welcoming cushions next to her storyteller. "Ennio insisted I read him when we were still at school." Evelina's eyes opened wide. "Are you telling me that the man who infected you with a demonic spirit was the Dracula of the monster movies?"

Saverio smiled. "Well, darling, Tepes was a well-known figure of history and the inspiration for Stoker's character, yes.

"I knew Stoker in his day," the vampire continued in an almost conversational fashion. "I became fascinated with him after he wrote his tome. I wanted to learn how he had discovered the truths he revealed in his stories. I traveled to London about fifty years ago and made myself known to him. We met and spoke at length several times over the course of a year or so. He knew what I was, and was as intrigued with me as I was curious about him. He welcomed the company of all manner of people, the more unconventional the better, as you may have deduced from his writings. He relished telling his stories, and I found that most of his information came from an acquaintance of his from Hungary by the name of Våmbéry. This Hungarian had traveled the world. He was quite an adventurer for a mortal, and I found that he knew of what he spoke when it came to the Order of the Dragon."

"Both Stoker and the Hungarian died not long after my interactions with the Dracula author. Lest you wonder, I had nothing to do with their departures from this life! I mention Stoker now in hopes that a bit of the truth hidden in his fiction may help you understand some events a bit better. Stoker's description of the vampyre having dominion over the wolf was a nod to the connection between the undead and the werewolf. Under the full moon, the werewolf is inhabited by the essence of the wolf. An undead being can be strengthened enough to survive a long famine, an ocean voyage, or a catastrophic injury by drinking the blood coursing through these mighty hounds, so we seek them out."

Saverio paused for an uneven breath and then he

explained again. "As many reasons as I had to kill Gaetano, even before the night he died, I could not do that to you, Evelina."

He added, "There is more in Stoker's yarn that may help you one day, mia amore. Keep the myth and the methodology of which he wrote in your mind."

Here Saverio stopped and sat looking ahead, hands in his lap. His breathing was a touch labored and awkward. It was obvious that he was drained. His tragic tale had been told.

But Evelina had one more question for her amante. She wiped at the tears brought on by the mention of Gaetano's agony and then inquired, "From where did the vampyre demons come in the beginning, Saverio? Do you know?" This was a question so old that no book she had yet read hinted at the answer. No metaphysician seemed to have an idea as to the origins of the invasion of the human plane by pernicious, blood-drinking spirits. Fiendish apparitions resembling vampyres had been spoken of in the Egyptian book of the dead, but the blood spirits of ancient Egypt were not like Saverio. They were ethereal entities that did not live in human bodies. Ennio had once said that the thread had been lost and he did not know if these ancient specters had anything to do with the monsters he and Evelina faced in the twentieth century. He had been, as of the last time he and Evelina had spoken about such things, unable to unearth the truth about Saverio's demon heritage.

Saverio did have an answer, or a theory anyway. "It was rumored in those ancient days, that Druid spells were the impetus for the first vampyre demon's escape from hell," he related. "It is my understanding that bandruí pagans summoned this first blood-draining demon. Their unwavering belief in the permanence of the human soul led some of them to resort to the black arts to conjure human specters. They even attempted to raise the dead, or so I was told. As is often the case, their practice allowed enemies that were never human to puncture the veil. The dark magicians found the thing they sought – an immortal spirit. But the deathless phantasm they raised was not an ancestral ghost. It was born of hell. It had not traversed the underworld to communicate or reassure the alchemists who freed it." Saverio's voice was failing and he whispered the last. "It came to spread chaos, destruction, and death."

Evelina leaned back into the cushiony sofa. As the clock ticked and the footsteps of neighbors living normal lives passed by her door, she mulled over all she had learned as Saverio sat quietly, waiting. She shed a tear as she thought, again, of her dear Gaetano and she prayed, once more, for his sweet soul. Her husband died an innocent and she knew that his immortal spirit did not need her prayers, but it comforted her to offer them. The hideous idea that, had he escaped, he might have had his throat opened in the violent clutch of a demon like the one that had murdered Annabella sickened her. She thanked God, finally, for the small blessing of his death not happening in that way.

She struggled to absorb all she had heard. Saverio's yarn was as astonishing as it was horrible and almost too much to take in at one sitting. Her mind still a jumble of questions, she eventually settled on the one that continued to rise to the surface. She reached out to Saverio as he studied his pale hands. Touching his cheek, she probed, "Saverio, did you save the soul of Vlad Tepes?"

"I don't know, Evelina," Saverio exhaled raggedly with his

newfound breath. "Was death his release or is he eternally damned for the atrocities he committed in his mortal life and under the vampyre curse? Tepes was a monster. He impaled his adversaries and drank their blood even when he was human. He built armies in life and built an army of the undead as well. It is a mystery to me. I do not know if Drago knew how great his sins were, nor do I know if he can ever be forgiven for them. I have no idea where his dirty soul now abides.

"I, myself, was a crusader for Christ. I killed in the name of my God. I now know this to be the greatest of sins but did not know it at the time. I have extinguished life again and again without mercy but now I have a conscience and am racked with guilt. Into this unaccountable bargain, I feel love." With these words, he looked at Evelina. In that look his love for her was evident. "Is it possible that my new and growing consciousness equals salvation for me? Is salvation attainable for one who has sinned as much, as long, as mortally as have I? Is the crushing guilt I feel penance enough for my centuries of mayhem? These are questions for which I have no answers, mia tesora Evelina."

He paused again to catch his reborn breath and then rushed on, his voice again laced with passion. "I do not know if I am any less culpable for my own great sins because I believed them to be just in life or because I was cursed in death. I do know this. I cannot live as a man even as I long for that almost more than I long for salvation. I want to make love to you ten thousand times. It is my most humble and heartfelt wish to be able to protect you for the rest of this life and centuries untold but this I cannot do." As he finished, he hung his head.

Tears flowed from Evelina's eyes in little rivers. "Please, can it not be so? Saverio, I will love you always. Let me take care of you."

"No, Evelina," he said, as he shook his lowered head from side to side.

Evelina wobbled a bit as she stood. Her eyes were wide as she grasped the full meaning of Saverio's words. She fairly shouted, "You are not asking me to kill you? You cannot!"

"We will need the help of the most reverend and most annoying one," said Saverio without emotion. Ennio had lost his Christian name once again.

"No, no, no, no," cried Evelina. "I won't do it, and I won't let Ennio destroy you, too. You are a man now. I love you. Please don't leave me. Live with me. Be alive *with* me!"

"Evelina, my Evelina. I am, indeed, a man at this moment. I am experiencing a sacred and profound love. That is more than I deserve, more than I ever dreamed I could have. I cannot offer you a lifetime. My cursed journey must be finished." His words were an entreaty, but she would not grant him his wish.

Sobbing, she flew into his arms. She begged him to stay with her. When she had said all she could think of to sway him she waited, listening to the wonder of her undead inamorato's breathing. Saverio held his peace as a long minute passed. She pulled away from him crying out again, "You cannot do this, Saverio, you *cannot!*"

Saverio eyes grabbed hers and held them as he swayed his head side to side. "No, my darling, I cannot. I must not." He pulled her back to him again. "But you can," he whispered.

Evelina pounded on the iron chest of her lover with both fists until she was worn out. Her breathing came in gasps as she gave up and slumped into his arms. As the minutes passed she became quiet in the vampire Saverio's arms and he leaned forward to her ear. His soft voice full of emotion he intoned, "Time and circumstance, even unto death, will never change my love for you, my Evelina." The human woman he loved looked up into his sad green eyes. He placed a most gentle kiss upon her forehead, then one on her cheek and then one on her expectant mouth. He covered her lips with his and stood. He carried her to the bed that was outfitted in simple, cool white cotton. There they made love slowly and deliberately. They surveyed and memorized every inch of one another. It was lovemaking meant to encompass the thousands of times that Saverio and Evelina would be denied the opportunity to be as one. The hours passed and Evelina forgot where her body left off and Saverio's began. As evening neared, exhausted in every conceivable way, she slept.

CHAPTER 27
THE HECATOMB

Rituals of decadent mortality
Are performed by confessors and widows
With instruments dull and unsparing
On centuries-old victims of Rome.

W hen Evelina opened her eyes, darkest night had fallen, and she was alone. There was a branch of wilting lilac on the pillow beside her. She had been covered up to her shoulders with the limp, white sheet.

It took her just a short while to awaken enough to remember all that had transpired that day. As the memories came flooding back to her, they did so with an accompanying sense of panic. Evelina kicked away the bed linen. Without dressing, she made a perfunctory search of the rooms. She did not expect to find Saverio, but she said an ardent though hasty prayer that she would. When she was certain that he had left her, she dressed hastily in slim pants and a loose blouse.

She rushed out into the night, neglecting to collect any kind of a wrap even though the mid-spring evening had grown brisk. Saverio had said that Ennio's help would be needed, so she ran in her girlish white sneakers straight to the church where her friend of old lived and prayed. He killed there, too, she reminded herself.

Evelina scrambled up the dusky slate steps of the church and threw herself at the heavy wood doors. They were locked. She did not waver before descending the steps two at a time and racing to the children's chapel door. The miniature sanctuary with its view of the altar through a glass wall had been left unlocked for emergency prayer for so long that, no doubt, the key with which to work its lock no longer existed. Evelina cursed herself for not having gone there first, as she rounded the corner of the rough stone church wall and threw open the crying room door.

What she saw through the wide glass window caused her to scream out "No!" so loudly that it vibrated the church bells that hung beside the door of the confined chapel. The tinkling chimes mocked Evelina's desperation. Her limbs trembled. Saverio, now beautifully human and able to do so without burning his alabaster skin, knelt, shirtless, before the tabernacle like a petitioner desirous of a blessing. *No,* thought the stricken Evelina, *like a sacrifice.* Ennio was at the altar as if reciting the mass. In his two hands, he held, thrust out before him, a long, shining sword with an ornate and bejeweled silver hilt.

At the sound of Evelina's scream, both men looked toward the room in which she was trapped. Ennio shot a look over to

Saverio on the gospel side of the church where the tabernacle resided. Saverio gestured to him and Ennio returned his eyes to the altar where his enormous red leather-bound gospel lay open. His lips started to move again with words he presumably saw on the page.

Evelina's eyes swept the room. She picked up a child-sized kneeler. The petite woman hefted the cumbersome thing over her head, held it there for a split second, and then threw it with all her might at the glass that separated her from the scene. The window shattered with a deafening tintinnabulation. Ennio stopped his chant. Saverio stood and turned toward Evelina who stepped through the window opening, kicking some pieces of broken glass out of her way. She strode forward, step by purposeful step until she stood inches from Saverio. She saw that the specter that continued to live within him was struggling to surface. His teeth lengthened and retreated. His full, pink face turned to a sallow and sunken death mask and then returned to life.

She faced him and said, "You must not do this to us. Do not leave me. How can you condemn me to a life of loving ghosts?"

Saverio grabbed Evelina's arms. His eyes now looked as she had first seen them, inflamed with green rage. "Look at me," he commanded. She could not have looked away had she wanted to. As she watched, Saverio's straight, white teeth turned to pointed fangs. His face transformed into a monstrous white mask. His eyes blazed like green torches. "Is this a man? Is this an eidolon you can love? Would you live with this? Would you have me live with this lurking beneath the surface of my humanity? I am a man, but one who has violated you and made you fear me. Evelina, my dearest love, I am a monster and my body may forever harbor this demon," Saverio snarled.

Evelina leaned forward and stretched on her tiptoes to place her smooth face against the waxy, white of Saverio's vampire cheekbone. "Yes," she whispered. "I love you, whatever you are and whatever secrets you hold in your soul. I need you. Please don't do this; don't go." Her voice was steady.

They stood like that, Saverio's vampiric visage held close to Evelina's soft, youthful cheek until the clock in the tower commenced striking the midnight hour. When the last gong faded, Saverio spoke with hushed intensity. "Mia amore, you must understand this. There was a time when the soulless creature you see before you would have turned you with your purest of hearts into a blood-sucking demon. It would have done so without a second thought, or the slightest feeling of sorrow. To know this, is agony for the man I almost am."

Ennio stood beside the ancient vampire now, his gleaming sword hanging by his side. He said quietly, "Let him go, Evelina. He is in unbearable pain. Cannot you of all people see that?"

Evelina turned to the priest. "Leave us, Ennio. Your thirst for blood is worse than any monster's," she hissed.

With these words, dark clouds of anger spread over Ennio's face. "Do you not recognize, Evelina, how much I care for you? You will never know how grateful I am to this man, and yes I know he is again a man, for bringing you safely through the horrors to which I have exposed you.

"Try to understand my dilemma. The last thing I want is to be the one to end his life now as it begins anew, the life of the soul-filled human he once was. But do you not see the depth of the ungodly affliction with which he, whom you profess to love, must live? I am trying to help him! How can you, you Evelina who weeps for the miseries of the smallest of God's creatures, not comprehend the abyss of this man's agony?"

Ennio implored her. "Do not try to stop this, Evelina. Do not interfere; help us! Mi amore, we need you. We need your strength."

Evelina's eyes, full of desperation, returned to Saverio's face. She watched as his vampiric features again retreated. "Is there no other way, my Darling?" she beseeched him. She turned to the priest, "Ennio, can't you find another way?"

"Trust me, mia carissima, I have tried and tried. I have searched the writings of every exorcist, every holy man, and every layperson who has ever collided with the undead and survived to tell the tale for an answer." Ennio studied the cursed man as he spoke. "Our Saverio is an anomaly. He has outlived all others of his kind. He is the strongest vampyre that has ever existed. There is no precedent for what we face here beyond that which he has set. It is entirely possible that no mortal man has ever had to live with the guilt he carries. His suffering is immeasurable, mia tesora. It is a wonder he is not mad already." Ennio rambled, trying desperately to make Evelina understand.

Saverio pulled his beloved close. He whispered in her ear. "I have always been strong, but I am at your mercy now. Grant me this chance for release. Perhaps it will, indeed, be my salvation. Don't deny me, Evelina. I found you in this life because I knew that you alone could love enough to do this." And then, so softly she almost didn't catch it, one more word. "Please."

Evelina pulled back. She saw tears forming in Saverio's eyes. It was the strongest evidence of his humanity and the depth of his sorrow that she had yet witnessed. As his shining jade eyes spilled over, and tears trickled down Saverio's face, a broken sob escaped his lips. His tender tears swayed her. By degrees, she backed away from his embrace pulling her arms from his. She turned to Ennio telling him with her sad, doe-like eyes that she would offer no more resistance.

Then she faced Saverio once more. "So be it, mio amore." Evelina's words were punctuated by her own anguished weeping. "I will not interfere. But I will not be a part of this."

Evelina turned away from the mysterious man with the flowing strawberry hair and the ever-changing eyes. She hobbled her way to the back of the church. Seizing the huge brass door handles, she remembered the locked doors and slid to the floor in defeat.

The two men turned away from Evelina, leaving her crumpled against the solid wooden doors and resumed the ritual they had begun as if there had been no interruption. Evelina paid only passing attention to Ennio's incantation but she realized the Latin words were not those of the Holy Mass. He spoke of blood. He spoke of lives taken, but also of hope, forgiveness, and justice for all victims. She moved first to her hands and knees and then, with effort, she stood as the echo of Ennio's words faded and the sanctuary grew quiet. The cleric descended the red marble altar steps toward Saverio with the hideous sword held aloft in his hands. Evelina clutched the back of one of the timeworn pews of the back row with both her hands. She squeezed with titanic force and a burning sensation surged up her arms and into her shoulders, neck, and jaw. Pain seared right into her brain, into her very mind, and it kept her from collapsing.

She watched, aghast, and squeezed harder still. Ennio raised his weapon high above the kneeling Saverio. Evelina closed her eyes and waited for the hiss of the sword cutting the air. What assailed her ears, though, was the ringing clatter of metal against marble. Just as the ear-splitting sound pierced the silence of the church, the back of the worn pew gave way. It crashed into the seat in front of it and splintered into several pieces.

Evelina's eyes flew open to see Ennio standing beside Saverio shaking his bent head from side to side, weeping like a child. "I cannot do it, mio amico. I am sorry. I want to stop the pain for you, but I cannot do this," he cried. "A mutant, a thing," he wailed, "I can slay in defense. I cannot kill a man with his arms spread before the Lord in supplication." The horrible sword lay, silent, by his feet.

Saverio shifted one foot to the floor and pushed himself to a standing position. He took a step forward and put his arms around the blubbering padre. "It is fine," he comforted. "Don't torture yourself, little man of God. All will be well." He dropped his arms and turned to face Evelina. She was placing one hand on a length of the broken pew back as with the other she pulled a long fragment of wood from the edge of it. She straightened and fixed her eyes on the vampire Saverio. She tottered her painstaking way up the center aisle of the church on legs weak and resistant.

She stopped when she was close enough to see each feature of the familiar face. Searching his jewel-like eyes one more time, she said, "I love you."

"If God can forgive, Evelina, we will be together again. My

love for you is stronger than death. It is stronger than hell," declared Saverio. His eyes held hers a moment longer and then he turned his back to her. Like a great phoenix about to take flight, he spread his arms out from his body. Without vacillation, Evelina raised the sharp length of wood. With both hands and a show of strength that belied her size, she drove it through Saverio's back and into his lost and broken heart. His body, omnipotent for centuries, crumpled to the floor. Evelina fell on top of it. She wept there with her arms around the inert form of her love until she could weep no more.

Saverio's body, to which human warmth had such a short while ago begun to return, grew cold again beneath Evelina's own. She had no sense of how long she had lain there on the altar when she felt two firm hands on her arms. Ennio lifted her and guided her away from the still corpse of her second lost adorato saying, "Go, my dear, courageous amica. I can finish this."

Evelina turned her back on the Gehenna of Saverio's liberation. This time, remembering the locked church, she stepped back through the jagged glass of the broken crying room window. She pushed open the door and walked out into the night. With no one to follow unseen protecting her along her path, she experienced a disturbing sensation of being exposed and vulnerable. Feeling more alone than she ever had before, but somehow more equipped to face the world's dangers, she wended her way back to the flat that was empty once again and absent of comfort save for the large, fragrant bouquet she would find unmoved from the counter.

CHAPTER 28
THE INITIATION

Enchanters, occultists, and seers
Conspire in temples and tombs,
With permission of specters and wraiths,
To slay chaos, possession, and doom.

Saverio's body was buried without its heart in the sanctified ground of the churchyard. Ennio judged a dolmen unnecessary. The caretaker of the church and church grounds helped Evelina plant a lilac bush beside the unembellished headstone that simply said: Saverio Tanicani – A Man of Faith.

Evelina spent the days of that summer on her knees in the churchyard, praying for the soul of her lost loves. She was able to conjure them even without the magic of the rosary beads she had clutched in her fist the first time she had seen Saverio; the first time he had saved her. She was so overpowered by the presence of her cruelly sacrificed husband or her enigmatic paramour on many of her visits, that she would see a shadow of one or the other just at the edge of her periphery. On such days she would remain motionless, soaking in the essence of that day's vision. If it were her young husband she detected, she would not move even to breathe because she had found that, if she started to turn her head, the loving spirit would, in one instant, dissipate to vaporous gauze.

When she perceived the spirit of Saverio, who had first died such a long time ago, she often glimpsed his thoroughly human features pass in front of her even if she did not stay one hundred percent still. When she did catch that momentary flash of the face of her ancient amante, though there was a smile upon it, there was a sadness to its visage. Because of the sorrow she detected in the spectral visage of the man whose mortal life she had ended, Evelina persevered in her prayers for his peace. At the same time, she was comforted by her visions of both her husband and the vampire she had loved because she did not detect any lingering malaise within the essence of either one. Both spirits felt free from the hardships of life and the tragedy of death.

One September day, kneeling in front of Saverio's quiet place of rest, Evelina sensed someone standing not in her periphery but behind her. She stood and spun around in one smooth motion expecting to catch a glimpse of her lost love. Today it was Ennio, solid, alive, and human though perhaps a bit thinner than he had been some months ago. He smiled at her, his blue eyes twinkling again, his black hair in its usual state of disarray, his priestly collar askew.

She could not help but return his smile even though the

two had yet to mend their relationship. Ennio said, "I have something for you."

"For me? What is it, Ennio?" she asked, her curiosity piqued. He reached into one pants pocket, did not find what he sought there, and tried another. At last, he came up with the gift. It was a cross about two inches long of white gold with yellow gold edges. Ennio reached out, placing the cross, with the fine gold chain to which it was attached, in Evelina's hand.

"It is lovely, Ennio. Thank you," she said, looking at him with surprised pleasure.

"It is not from me." Ennio looked straight into Evelina's eyes as he replied.

"Oh," Evelina breathed. "To protect me because he cannot?" she guessed.

"Yes. Gold, he said, was stronger than silver and just as effective at warding off the unhallowed when it is in the shape of a cross. He beseeched me to hold on to it for a time when I could present it to you without exacerbating your grief to a great degree. I hope I have waited long enough." Uncertainty showed on Ennio's face as he spoke.

"It is fine, Ennio, it is good. I thank you for your care," Evelina reassured him. "Although," she contemplated, "I feel that we may have gotten the message a bit wrong. It is not only to protect me because he cannot. I know it will be helpful in that way but the cross, I believe, is to remind me that he always will be there when I need him to be."

Evelina, her eyes misting, opened the clasp and arranged the piece of jewelry around her neck. She placed one hand under the cross, lifting her chin to present her new pendant to her oldest friend for inspection. She smiled at him. She knew that there was a great deal for she and Ennio to work out, but it seemed to Evelina, at that moment, almost as if things between them were once again as they had been before Gaetano's death.

Ennio looked where Evelina's hand indicated and said, "It is just right." As she adjusted the cross at her throat, he reached up and took her hand in his. Looking into her eyes, he said, "What are your plans for the days to come, my brave and esteemed warrior?"

Evelina broke his earnest gaze. She looked at the ground and sighed. "Ennio, I have spoken to Mother Angelica. I am going to enter the convent." She stated this firmly, but Ennio's reaction caused her confidence to wane. He laughed aloud among the dead and it exasperated her that she felt certain others laughing along with him.

She gave Ennio a defiant look as he wiped his eyes of the tears his outburst had caused. "I am sorry, Evelina," he said. "I do not mean to dismiss your faith or impugn your sincerity. You would be a sister like no other with gifts possessed by no bride of Christ I have ever known or of whom I have heard tell."

"I know you want to care for the little ones, and you shall as you always have," Ennio continued. "You will not be doing so as a Sister of Mercy, however. I will talk to Mother Angie, myself if I must," he warned. His tone softened. He urged, "Walk with me. I will tell your fortune."

Curiosity compelled Evelina to walk along beside her friend and priest through the rows of headstones. She looked over at him and said in a haughty voice dripping with sarcasm, "Fine, Ennio, you tell me what it is that *you* think I will be doing with my interminable future." She was angry with him once again. She would be the one to decide her fate, and if she wanted to join the sisters, she would do so. She knew Mother Angelica well enough to know that the stolid nun would not be ordered about or swayed by any man, ordained or layman, no matter how much clout he had.

But Ennio had plans. "You, the White Witch of Rome, will again be my assistant. Or I should say, I will be yours. Our collaboration will be in, well, let us say, a semi-official capacity," he suggested. "Your knowledge and your wisdom, not to mention your unmatched strength and courage cannot stay locked away, my dearest one. Prayer is prayer. You will pray as much," he reconsidered, "no, you will pray much more from the places you will visit than you would if you were cloistered away with the virtuous Sisters."

Evelina took a deep breath but did not introduce an argument.

Ennio took advantage of her hesitation to continue. "There is much evil in the world, Evelina. I do not need to convince you of all people of this sad truth. You have a unique understanding, gleaned from your experiences, that is needed to combat the forces that would ravage all that is good and right. The Sisters fight corruption with their prayers. We are God's instruments too. He will use us to answer those prayers. It is your duty and your mission in this life, just as it is mine. It has been ordained by God. He has shown this to us in no uncertain terms.

Evelina and Ennio stopped of one accord and faced each other. "Oh, Ennio, can we ever truly save anyone?" Evelina sighed.

"Evelina, Evelina," Ennio sounded as if he were astonished by her question. "You have done so! Saverio interceded for your life more than once but in return, I believe you saved his very soul. Our poor Gaetano. He was blameless, but we saved him from himself. We saved, too, the untold others we shielded from his attacks. Like ripples from a tiny pebble thrown into the sea, we may have rescued hundreds."

"And so has Saverio," the clergyman asserted, "because in those sad months after the horrible departure of our dear Gaetano, Saverio was relating to me events of the past. He was educating me. He helped me to separate facts from myth in a more concrete way than has anything I have found in the Vatican's athenaeum of horrors. The text that I wrote with his help will be one that demon hunters of the future will rely upon to defeat a legion of malignant entities. It will preserve innumerable lives."

Evelina looked into the kind face of her alter ego of old. Her anger had dissolved with his words and been carried away with the same temperate autumn breeze. With one hand, she worried the gold cross as she spoke in earnest tones, "I hear what you are saying. I will not pretend it doesn't make sense to me. I must apologize to you, Ennio. I have held you responsible for events that God alone can explain. I know that you did all that you could for my Gaetano and all that you could for Saverio." Ennio was shaking his head but she went on. "I have missed you. I feel supremely guilty for abandoning you. Please tell me that you forgive me."

"Oh, Evelina, mia compagna. There is nothing to forgive. I failed you. I failed Gaetano and Saverio. Your anger with me is utterly righteous. I know that my prodding and my expectations would, as Saverio himself once told me, try the patience of a saint."

Evelina could not help but smile at the image of Saverio chastising Ennio for his persistence.

Ennio went on, "I am the one who must seek forgiveness from you, my dearest friend, for leaving you to do that for which I lacked the courage. You accomplished, on my behalf, the thing that is the precise definition of my calling. You helped Saverio preserve his soul. It would not have happened without your intercession, just as Saverio predicted." Her priest's eyes welled, and Evelina could not keep her own tears from spilling out. She reached out and grasped Ennio's arms in her two hands. It was the most intimate gesture the two had engaged in for some time, and Evelina delighted in the comfort of it.

"Let us leave the judgments to God, Ennio, my old friend," she consoled her priest. "We have castigated ourselves enough. We each did the best that we could. You are right, I think, that we both are meant to use our God-given attributes to fight the wickedness that makes its way into our world. Our gifts are not the same. Yours is to sense evil and not be deterred. Mine is to see the humanity in each person and not shy away from love."

She released his arms and held her hands palm up in a gesture that said, *There you have it.*

"What about that day in the catacombs, Evelina?" Ennio reminded her. "You saw the malignancy there. It had a great effect on you."

Evelina tilted her head and, with a sad smile, explained to her old friend, "No, Ennio. It was not the evil of the sinners interred in those caves that depleted me and compelled me to flee. It was their suffering."

Ennio beamed at the guileless, loving woman as she went

on. "Perhaps the great lesson for us in all of this, my darling one, is that no one can face the challenges of life alone, that our human connection is everything. We knew that once. We knew it when we were children and beyond. But over these last few months, I have forgotten. I am exceedingly sorry." She was quiet for a brief interval and then, again with a stroke of her hands on the black sleeve of the rector's everyday garb, she petitioned, "Wait here for just a minute or two. Will you do that?"

Ennio nodded. Evelina knew he watched as she turned to make her way back to the grave of her demon beloved. There she spoke to the air around her. "Oh, Saverio, my Saverio; I feel that you would have me do what Ennio asks of me. I know that you will, in some form, be there to assist us through the knowledge you have given or, perhaps, even in some mystical way if it is God's will. Know that I will pray without ceasing for you for the rest of my life no matter what awful adventures our 'annoying little priest' drags me into." She smiled a small smile and then passion made its way into her voice as she continued. "I will love you always. I will do this thing and if I can help anyone at all, it will be done on *your* behalf. It will be your penance, the penance you did not have the opportunity to perform."

It was the colorful fall, and leaves covered the neatly-trimmed graves. Only the chrysanthemums bloomed. It should not have been possible, but in the breeze that came up as she spoke these words, Evelina detected the scent of lilacs along with a hint of spice that took her back to the last time she had held Saverio in her arms.

She smiled more contentedly then. Taking a long, deep breath of the fragrant air around her, she turned and walked to Ennio who was faithfully waiting for her at the iron gates of the peaceful church graveyard. As she reached him, they began to walk together again. Evelina, the brave white witch, and spiritual warrior gave one more big sigh and said, "I suppose I must say that I am 'in'. What now, my dear holy man?"

"Well." Ennio straightened and announced, "our first adventure will be a trek to America, to 'The States', as they say."

Evelina had heard rumors of disturbing and grievous problems coming to the fore in the American church. She supposed Ennio was to be dispatched to offer guidance to church leaders there. Or perhaps he was to use his particular talents to suss out evil among the American clergy? "What will be my role in your new endeavors, Ennio?" she probed. "Am I to be your secretary?"

"No, no, mia amico! Together we will perform a rite of exorcism." Evelina stopped in her tracks, a look of incredulity on her face. "Oh come now, Evelina, mia cara," said Ennio with a grin. He administered a playful clap to Evelina's shoulder. "There is nothing to fear. It is only a demon; just like our Saverio."

The End

www.ingramcontent.com/pod-product-compliance
Lightning Source LLC
Chambersburg PA
CBHW021043130626
46552CB00005B/1984